MENDED AND MARKED

WARRIOR ELITE SERIES BOOK 6

V.T. BONDS

Copyright © 2022 by V.T. Bonds

Cover design by V.T. Bonds

All rights reserved.

No part of this book may be reproduced in any form or by any electronic or mechanical means, including information storage and retrieval systems, without written permission from the author, except for the use of brief quotations in a book review.

This story is knot for the faint of heart. It is a dark action-packed Omegaverse story set in a world where violence and sexual situations occur. Scenes are not glossed over. Sensitive readers please abstain.

Dedication

I'm still breathing. So are you.
We win.
Don't let anyone tell you otherwise.

TABLE OF CONTENTS

Dedication	3
Table Of Contents	5
Chapter One	7
Chapter Two	15
Chapter Three	29
Chapter Four	45
Chapter Five	57
Chapter Six	67
Chapter Seven	79
Chapter Eight	91
Chapter Nine	99
Chapter Ten	111
Chapter Eleven	123
Chapter Twelve	133
Chapter Thirteen	145
Chapter Fourteen	157
Chapter Fifteen	169
Chapter Sixteen	179
Chapter Seventeen	189
Chapter Eighteen	201
Chapter Nineteen	213
Chapter Twenty	227
Chapter Twenty-One	237
Keep up with V.T. Bonds	247

Chapter One

Duri

The vast openness of space locks me in amazement and holds me hostage until footsteps pull my attention away from the massive viewing window.

"Still standing here, Du?"

I smile and bat Seung's hand away, years of friendship teaching me to expect his teasing tug on my hair.

"Of course. It's so… mesmerizing. It makes me feel small."

"You *are* small, Duri—except for that belly of yours."

His light tone and soft chuckle take the sting out of his words, but I tilt my head away to hide my blush. My hands lift and caress the swell of my expanding waistline, protecting the new life growing in my womb.

I don't have any immediate words to toss back at him. It's my fault I'm carrying his offspring: if I had elected to suffer through my heat alone instead of asking him to tend me, I wouldn't be pregnant.

But I can't feel shame for such a gift. It's precious, even if its father and I will only ever be friends. I fill my lungs until they ache and offer him my brightest smile.

"It'll get bigger, you know. I'm not even halfway through the pregnancy yet."

"Ew, Du. You sure know how to make an alpha cringe. Go on to the medical bay then, while my offering is still fresh."

Trying to hide how much his playful words hurt, I force my smile bigger and pat his arm as I step around him.

"Thanks, Seung. You didn't have to come, much less offer more services, so I'm truly grateful."

He shrugs and turns toward the expanse of nothingness, causing an ache to pulse behind my sternum.

We spoke at length and signed a contract before my heat began, so I know he holds no regrets over our rutting and subsequent child, but his dismissal still hurts.

With a heavy heart, I start the trek to the medical bay, keeping close to the wall despite the wide hallway. The same worries I've carried for years seem to weigh heavier than ever before, but I bear them as best I can.

Each step offers me another moment of newness. Another moment of motherhood, even if I haven't met my baby yet. I shake off my troubling thoughts and sneak my hand to the bottom curve of my belly, excitement bubbling within me.

When a shape no taller than my protruding belly button darts out of a room as I pass, I squeak and flail, trying my best to keep my feet under me.

I fail, landing on my hands and knees. As sharp pain lances through my arms and legs, a tall, curvy shape steps from the same room, her shout ringing in my ears.

"Oh no! Are you alright?"

Her husky voice sounds more harried than worried, and through the haze of pain I realize it must have been her child I almost squashed. The patter of tiny feet scurrying down the hall awakens my own maternal instincts.

Gritting my teeth, too shaken and embarrassed to form words, I sit back and nod while gesturing for her to follow her youngling.

"I'm sorry. He just got his cast removed, but it's no excuse. Hayden, get back here right this instant!"

Little feet don't even pause as they round the corner. His mother takes off after him, leaving me to rise on my own. Casting a glance around the hall as I use the wall to stand, I shake my head and thank the gods there was no one else around to share my embarrassment. I brush my knees with shaky fingers and check my palms. With the smooth floor and short distance, only a light blue bruise forms on the heel of my right palm where a blood vessel popped from the impact. I don't bother to lift my skirt to look at my knees—I already know two new bruises form over my kneecaps, joining the myriad of other scrapes and bruises.

Who would have thought a slightly unlucky person could turn into an outright clutz with the change in balance pregnancy brings?

Sighing at myself, I hurry down the hall with as even a gait as I can manage, not stopping until I reach room number six. I slide my passenger card across the reader and twist the handle after it turns green. The overhead lights turn on as I step into the room, revealing the examination table along the far wall, the privacy screen in the corner, and the row of medical equipment built into the left wall.

A tray of instruments sits beside the temperature-controlled container at the foot of the table. I flip the lock on the door and limp across the room. After opening the container and pulling out the hot bottle and cellophane wrapped pill, I quickly shut the lid and set the bottle on the tray. With careful fingers, I unwrap the massive egg-like pill and cram it in my mouth before grabbing the bottle and sucking down the hot water as fast as possible. If it weren't for the oily coating on the casing of the pill, it wouldn't fit down my throat. Even so, I fight to choke it down.

The struggle proves worth it as the casing dissolves and releases my best friend's seed into my stomach. A tiny limb bops my internal organs as my womb dweller dances in delight over the natural nutrients. I smile, enjoying the sensation for a moment before sucking in a breath and climbing onto the table.

A shudder rolls through the room, making me pause, but when nothing else seems out of the ordinary, I settle my rump on the table and swallow my discomfort. My cheeks heat as my pulse echoes between my legs, the incessant ache of lust never far away since pregnancy causes my hormones to run high.

Ignoring the raised heat on my face, knowing a blush paints my cheeks red, I pull the cylinder from the container, fit it into the speculum resting on the tray, and hike my skirt up. With my heels braced on the edge of the table, I slide the cold metal between my labia, still uncomfortable with the process even though I've done it almost every other day for almost twenty weeks. Unable to stop the trembling of my hand and the subsequent tightening of my body at the intimate touch, I insert the tool and deploy the plunger until it clicks. Pressure grows deep within my channel as the synthetic plug expands, fitting itself above my pubic bone where an alpha knot would expand. I shift my hand to remove the speculum and gasp as the table vibrates under me.

Gravity shifts as I yank the tool from between my legs. My back slams into the wall and my feet slip off the edge of the table as the entire ship jerks.

The lights flicker.

With the calming warmth of Seung's seed infiltrating my insides, my brain struggles to understand the significance of the changes. I push my skirt down over my knees and blink at the video projected on the wall, an odd detachment making it take several moments for me to realize it's an announcement from the cruise's captain.

Wrapping my arms around my midsection, I force my brain to focus on the captain's words.

"—entering the atmosphere in twenty seconds. I say again, use only the escape pods on decks three and four. All individuals on decks one and two, strap into the nearest safety seat. Prepare for a crash landing."

Even as the overhead lights turn a flashing red and sirens blare, I stare in mute shock at the elderly man's face.

Is this a joke?

The table jolts underneath me.

No, not a joke, and even if it is, I can't take the risk of ignoring the signs.

Almost falling to my knees as I jump off the table, I stagger to the emergency seats built into the corner of the room. My hands attack the straps the second my butt hits the surface, fumbling and fighting until the harness rests against my chest. I smash the red button on the armrest and wince as the straps tighten against my torso, but I reach upward and yank the shield down until it clicks into place at the end of the armrest. A second see-through barrier rises from the floor and seals itself to the first, fully encasing me and the empty chair next to me in a small misshapen room.

The captain's face remains on the screen until the power flickers, the strobe lighting lasting for several seconds until everything goes pitch black. Not even the emergency lights turn on. For terrifying, endless seconds, I sit alone. My skull squeezes my brain until I worry my eyeballs will pop out of my skull. I hug my stomach, praying for help, desperate to protect my youngling.

I want them to survive more than anything in the universe. They're mine. I love them.

Needing to block out the sirens and horrible jerking of the craft, I whisper to the new life in my belly, telling them over and over how much I need them. How much I love them. How I'll do everything I can to protect them, if only they'll stay strong while chaos strikes.

With a deafening boom, my senses explode into fragmented nonsense as the ship meets land. The vast emptiness of space invades my thoughts, stealing me away from the present and holding me hostage in darkness.

Yet even here, pain finds me. I hurt. I hurt in too many places. My head. My spine. My legs.

But not my abdomen. Held securely to the seat and protected from the worst of the impact by the shields, the new life growing in my womb swims in the seed of an alpha they may never meet again.

Wetness seeps down my face.

Chapter Two

Cahress

White-hot agony shoots into my knuckles and up through my wrist. I ignore the pain and grab the barrel with my other hand, using my attacker's own momentum to propel him closer to me. With pins and needles pricking up and down my arm, I lift my forearm and bring it crashing down on the black clad limb so hard bones crack.

The puny ISC guard dies screaming as I pull my blade from my chest harness and bury it in his throat. Crimson sprays in a wide arc as I yank my knife free of him, letting him free fall to the ground with a wet thump.

Adrenaline floods my veins, urging me to fall into instinct, but I use my years of training and stay firmly in control of my motions. Wiping the filthy blade on my water-resistant suit, I slide it back into its holster and stalk forward.

"Well, if they didn't already know we're here, they do now," Thret rumbles, stepping around me and sending me an angry glance. I roll my shoulders and force my dense fur to settle, knowing Thret thinks of nothing beyond the mission. His thick, bony plates reflect the soft yellow light from the floorboards, causing his silhouette to shift through the shadows.

"I don't hear an alarm, and it's not like *he* had enough time to sound one."

At my retort, Commander Ru'en snarls and stalks forward. His white pupils narrow in his black irises, relaying his annoyance.

"We can't take chances, Cahress. These ISC bastards are too conniving. Take the rear."

His shoulder grazes mine as he passes, chilling my skin despite our temperature regulated suits. A rare Frigent, Commander Ru'en's blood runs like liquid ice in his veins—even through both of our suits he sucks the heat right out of my flesh.

Usually he doesn't run so cold, but a few weeks ago another Warrior Elite pummeled him into the ground, turning the normally grim alpha into a cruel beast. With the added adrenaline of our mission, he pulls all traces of warmth from the air, creating an almost visible cloud of icicles around him.

Commander Ru'en strides past Thret and leads the way down the darkened hall, his footsteps eerily silent on the backlit floor panels.

Thret follows him on equally quiet feet.

Jokur taps my shoulder. The dark markings around his eyes camouflages well in the dim lighting, but my keen eyesight sees him point at himself then motion toward the rear, letting me know he wants me to go in front. I nod and follow Thret.

We haven't heard anything from Choku, which is a blessing. His special skills make him the perfect candidate for sneaking to the other side of the mountain and securing any potential exits. If he hasn't contacted us via our suits' communication units, then we don't have to worry about ISC reinforcements showing up out of nowhere, like they did when Warrior Elite Team 1 began the first invasion of an ISC facility on this planet, Mai'CuS.

I dart across the first doorway and keep my attention trained further down the hall, waiting for Commander Ru'en and Thret to clear the room. They exit empty-handed with the scent of death clinging to their suits.

The moment they exit the room, I continue to the nearest doorway and check the surrounding wall for hidden cameras or traps and swipe the hacked chip hidden in my wristband across the card reader. I surge forward, entering the room before the door fully opens, and lunge across the space. My knife pierces the beta's temple before he finishes sitting up. He falls back onto the bed and jerks as I slice his throat. Several seconds later, he lies as still as death. A quick perusal of the room shows no other beings within, so I wave Jokur out and follow him into the hall.

Only three other doors remain—one on the left, one on the right, and the reinforced door at the end of the hall.

Commander Ru'en glares at me, relaying his unhappiness over my disobedience—because how dare I not be last in formation—before he unlocks the last door on the right and disappears into the darker room. Thret follows him in, an unnecessary precaution, but we don't take chances.

For over a decade we've fought together in the worst places. We've killed innumerable foes and done unspeakable deeds, yet we've also saved countless innocent souls, including most of my family, in our war against the ISC.

The largest scientific body across the known galaxies, the ISC hides in plain sight. They began long ago as a company intended for good, but over time, they became corrupt. Entire branches do as they wish, mostly without recourse, using the funding and support of the company to conduct vile experiments. We've encountered horrifying scenes and conditions over the years, but every time we questioned personnel, the answer has always been the same.

No one knows who leads the evil branches of the ISC. Cut off one leader's head and two more rise to take their place.

My teammates and I each began our own quests to rid the galaxy of ISC scum on our own terms, but when we one-by-one crossed paths, we knew we'd never find a better team. Commander Ru'en has a mind created for tactics, even with his grumpy façade, and I trust him with my life. I know I'll never find a better leader.

He exits the room and falls in behind Jokur as I approach the last barracks room. A quick sweep of the surroundings, swipe of my wristband, and silent attack later, and my team remains the only living creatures within the narrow hall.

Nestled in the caves of a barren mountain range, this facility should only hold a few rooms beyond the reinforced door. We had no clue tiny compounds like this existed until a few weeks ago—right after Commander Ru'en got his ass beat by a fellow Warrior Elite from Team 1.

The concept of tiny pockets of evil tucked anywhere along the surface of the planet is terrifying and daunting, especially since we intend to stay on Mai'CuS for the rest of our lifespans.

Almost a decade ago, we met a convincing and talented omega spy, Commander Minette, and her war bred alpha, Commander Draukir. They pitched their spiel of intentions and won our loyalty by proving their skills.

Our common enemy—the ISC—and the threat to our peoples brought us here. We need a place to live in safety. Mai'CuS will be that place.

We must rid it of pests first, which is why we're infiltrating this compound in the middle of the night, with no backup beyond our own skills.

With every room devoid of life, Commander Ru'en approaches the heavy metal door.

My gut tightens, the familiar sense of dread infecting my chest and sending tingles down my spine. It weighs down the tip of my tapered tail, but I flex my muscles and force it into a ready position.

Nothing good ever hides behind doors locked by the ISC. I can only pray that whatever lies beyond remains healthy enough for medical care or is already dead.

Instinct tells me we won't be that fortunate this time.

Using a fallen guard's key card, Commander Ru'en unlocks the door and cracks it open. He stands, poised to strike, with less than an inch between the door and the frame. Several seconds tick by as we remain on high alert, listening for any alarms or signs of trouble. When none arise, we stalk forward on silent feet, leaving a few yards between each of us for safety's sake.

The fluorescent lighting makes the white walls and floor painfully bright. I shift my knife within my grasp, getting a better hold on the hilt as my heart thuds against my breastbone.

Faint wails leak through the two doors, the sound growing louder as we stalk closer. Commander Ru'en and Thret head to the furthest vestibule, while Jokur and I crouch on either side of the unassuming door over halfway down the long hall.

More than three voices create the endless sounds of agony, and although none of us show it, the pain infects our hearts.

Commander Ru'en taps his own shoulder and crouches low. Three seconds later, Thret and I use key cards we took from the ISC guards we murdered to open the doors and rush in.

Crimson colors my vision.

Strapped to a chair in the middle of the room sits a broken omega. Patches of her skin look blacker than barbecue while thin vertical lines on her torso, face, and limbs seep blood. Though sheared to her scalp in several places, what remains of her hair sports caked blood and other unmentionable substances.

A human alpha, covered head to toe in white, wields a thin surgical instrument as he hovers over her.

I fling my arm and watch as my knife somersaults through the space between us. It sinks into his bicep and forces him to drop his weapon. His subsequent shout ends on a wet gurgle as I yank a second knife from my chest harness and lunge across the room, burying my blade between his face shield and chest protection. Dark red liquid spews from his neck in a wide arc as I kick his stomach, keeping my knife tight in my grip.

The wailing doesn't stop. It surrounds me, bombarding me from both sides and sending streaks of pain into my soul.

An emaciated form lies curled on the bed, barely more than sallow flesh wrapped around frail bones. A machine whirs near the head of the threadbare mattress, an ugly brown liquid flowing through the clear tubes and into the human's arm.

She screams in time with the bound omega, their sounds of misery so in sync my own heart quails at the implication.

When I step toward the husk of a human on the bed, Jokur finishes checking the corners of the room before approaching the omega in the chair. I don't hesitate, sensing how little time these individuals have left to live if they don't receive proper medical care.

Reading the dials and switches on the machine leaves me with more questions than answers, so I squat down next to the bed and take off the top half of my mask, keeping the bottom half sealed over my nose and mouth in case of an airborne attack.

"Look at me."

The woman does not stop screaming. I touch the back of her hand, only to yank back in horror when blood bursts from her flesh.

Jokur yells. I turn. The omega's hand bleeds freely. Bile rises in my throat as I realize her new injury sprouts from where I touched the female on the bed.

"Shit! What do we do?" Jokur puts my own thoughts into words. Movement from the corner of my eye makes me surge to my feet, ready for whatever attack may come.

The large, rectangular frame embedded into the far wall morphs to a mirror before becoming opaque, revealing the room beyond.

An alpha stands strapped to a torture device in the center of the room, facing the frame. Three white clad corpses lay in heaps on the floor while Commander Ru'en and Thret stand on either side of the high-tech torture device.

"We get them out of here. That's what we do," Commander Ru'en demands in a tight voice.

A few heavy seconds pass as we gather our mental defenses.

"The female on the bed cannot be touched."

I point to their hands, including the alpha's identical wound in the gesture.

"We'll do what we can. Provide quick first aid and prep them for travel. We can't stay."

Jokur curses and squats down in front of the chair as Thret pivots to stand in front of the unknown alpha, their movements quick and efficient as they take off the top of their helmets and pull out their first aid kits.

I follow suit, returning my attention to the woman on the bed. She resembles a skeleton more than a human, so sick I can't tell if she's omega or beta.

Glancing over my shoulder as I grab my first aid kit, I grit my teeth as silence sits heavy in the terror-filled air. Knowing Commander Ru'en won't approve, I ease a comforting rumble through my chest.

"Hi, little female. You don't know me, but I'm here to take you away from here."

Cloudy eyes meet mine and her mouth opens, but no sound comes out. With steady hands despite the fury and fear swirling through my chest, I turn off the machine and crimp the line a few inches above her port before cutting the tube with the tiny, sterile pair of scissors in my kit. Keeping my gloves away from her flesh, I secure the end of the line to her forearm with a loose bandage. As I slide my attention to her bleeding hand, all chaos breaks loose.

One moment limp, the next seizing, she jerks and writhes so hard the bed shakes despite being bolted to the floor. Thick brownish blood pours from her hand, mouth, and eyes, the gory scene made worse as her flesh tears open with each movement. I press her into the mattress with a forearm across her shoulders and thighs, trying to protect her from herself, but she's lost to the world.

She stops moving. Stops breathing. Stops bleeding.

With my emotions in turmoil but my body locked tight within my cold control, I rise and discover the other two victims in the same state—dead.

There's too much blood soaked into the mattress for any hope of resuscitation.

"Drag or burn?" Thret asks without emotion.

I grit my teeth and ignore the memories flashing through my mind's eye. Time and time again I find myself in similar horror and time and time again I make it through by the tip of my tail.

"Burn."

Mended and Marked

Commander Ru'en's decision fills me with both relief and horror. Dragging bloody corpses through the mountains holds zero appeal but setting the bodies on fire always sends the weight of finality through my soul.

Needing no other instruction since we've spent years completing missions together, we move in unison, pulling little oblong discs from our belts and placing them in opposite corners of the room. I toss my detonator to Jokur and stalk into the hall, keeping my gait even and senses alert despite the sludge roiling in my stomach.

Such evil leaves a stain on the soul, even after a decade of exposure.

I slide the top half of my mask back into place and set my sights on the outer door. Wanting nothing more than to feel the cool, fresh air shifting through my thick, tan undercoat, I squash the desire and continue forward, pushing through the reinforced door and entering the first room on the right. After placing a disk in the far corner, I exit into the hall and follow Thret as he heads toward the outer door, his second explosive already placed in the second room on the right.

Jokur joins our procession after placing his disc in the room on the opposite side of the hall. Commander Ru'en brings up the rear, catching Jokur's detonator after he tosses it over his shoulder.

The outer door swings open at Thret's vicious shove, slamming against the jagged wall of the cave so hard the metal warps. He sprints the last three steps before lunging into the darkness.

I follow him, throwing my body over the lip of the cave and free falling for a few glorious moments. I wish I could enjoy the wind ruffling my dense pelt, whistling through my whiskers, and streaming over the broad base of my tail, but my suit provides a necessary barricade between myself and the world. I reach out and grab a shallow outcropping. Swinging my momentum sideways into a wide arc, I release the handhold and jump from jagged rock to jagged rock until the mountains rise to cover the lightening sky.

As the first light of dawn teases the horizon, I leap one last time, propelling my body over the maze of deadly boulders along the outer rim of the mountain range and fall for long moments until my boots thud against hard-packed clay. Sprinting forward, I move out of Jokur's landing spot but stay close to the base of the large stone boulder.

Behind us lies death and misery, hidden within cold stone.

Ahead of us lies the vast emptiness of sand and sky, and a future littered with more pain.

As Commander Ru'en lands on the baked clay, a flash of light erupts on the horizon. We turn as one, homing in on the abnormality. Just north of where the sun should rise from the desert, flames eat at what can only be a space craft.

Our boots pound against the dry, cracked land as we head toward the wreckage. Despite our suits regulating the air within, the moment the sun crests the dunes, sweat trickles down my back. My heart hammers so hard against my breastbone I almost miss Commander Ru'en's discussion with base camp through our communicators.

Even though my life consists of nothing except darkness, a thicker sense of dread pulls me toward the crash. My heart demands I move faster, the miles between my body and the explosions too many. For what, I don't know, but the draw yanks me onward until my thighs ache and my pulse pounds in my ears.

I can't fail again today.

My instincts tell me too much is at stake, even if my mind has no idea why.

Chapter Three

Duri

Smoke fills my nostrils as the shield opens. I lift my heavy eyelids and push away the white covered hands reaching for me, disoriented and confused. Flames lick along my vision while crumpled metal and white beasts fill the rest.

Nothing makes sense. Everything hurts. Something in my abdomen shifts and flutters against my other organs.

Snapping into reality, I stop fighting the hands trying to free me from the seat and join in their efforts. My fingers fumble in a mad scramble, desperate to get out of the restraints, so when fat digits gather my wrists and pull them aside, I don't struggle despite the painful grip.

The harness finally releases, but the hand doesn't let go of my arms. I look up into my savior's face mask and see nothing but my own frantic and frazzled eyes reflected back at me.

Unease crawls up my sore spine.

The form seems to be human, but he must be alpha—an alpha much bulkier than the males on my home planet—and his strength proves more than anyone I've ever encountered before. He yanks me onto my feet with ease and stoops down as though to throw me over his shoulder.

Instinct kicks in. My knee jerks upward, but I lose my balance since my head swims and my natural clumsiness amplifies my instability.

"No! I'm pregnant!"

The white-clad form pauses before reaching into his pocket and slapping a thin band around my wrists. I cough from the mixture of smoke and surprise and struggle in earnest when he lifts me off my feet and plasters me to his chest. With his hold trapping my hands between us and his nearness preventing me from kneeing him, my struggles prove useless as he stomps through the wreckage.

The smoke proves to be too much. I sag in his arms, taking comfort in knowing he's getting me out of immediate danger, and cough until fresh air surrounds us. I suck it down but cough harder, my throat raw and gritty while my lungs feel scorched.

A group of survivors huddle together a few feet away from the flames, but I can't see much beyond the bulky arms encasing me. It isn't until my rescuer stalks past them that I realize a vehicle trains its headlights on them, pinning them in place.

He ignores their cries for help and continues into the darkness. A tan, wheeled vehicle flashes across my narrowed vision as he carries me past it, not stopping until we reach the back.

I struggle to find my balance when he sets me down, but two cruel hands grab my biceps from behind and hold me still, their grip so tight my fingers tingle from restricted blood flow.

"Tag and process. She's a prime candidate for study 229C."

The male's strange accent makes my senses reel until I register his words. He nods at the person holding me before turning and striding back into the flames, his footfalls echoing in my head as though he stomps on my skull.

Another large male in a white suit steps around me and reaches for my neck. I flinch but can't move away. My bones may bruise from the terrible grip on my arms. Cold, rough leather wraps around my throat before the alpha in front of me snaps the collar closed and drops into a squat. Two seconds later, similar bands squeeze my upper thighs, my stomach heaving at having a stranger so close to my intimates. His glove caresses my knee as he releases the hem of my skirt, letting it fall back to my ankles.

"Stop! Please!"

Too little too late, I find my voice. It hurts to speak, and I sound hoarse, but I struggle without effect.

A needle sinks into my flesh above the brutal grip on my right bicep.

No medicine rushes into my system.

"Tagged. Toss her into slot three."

The ground shifts underneath my slippers as the person holding my shoulders pulls me backward. I dig in my heels and realize sand covers the planet as far as my eyes can see. A detached part of me notices the sun rising above the horizon and wonders at how glorious the colors of sunrise are in this world.

I don't know where we are, but I do know we aren't where we're supposed to be. No planet on the cruise's itinerary had a desert this large, and I've never seen anyone wear all-white suits like these, either.

The hands pull me toward the pitch-black mouth of the vehicle's back door.

"No! Let me go!"

Stronger this time, but still pitiful and shrill, my voice grinds in my throat.

"Duri!"

I barely glimpse Seung's striking face before the relentless hands push me into the vehicle. Agony streaks into my shoulder as I trip and land on the hard floor, but I breathe through the pain and try to curl into a ball to protect the delicate life within my womb.

Sounds of scuffle filter through the opening, but the alpha grabs me again and hauls me upward. I fight, but he clips my bound hands to a chain bolted to the wall and pushes my shoulder so hard I have no choice but to sit on the built-in bench. He pulls a strap over my thighs and secures me to the hard surface.

The last time I was restrained, I was too far into my heat to care about the bindings. Now, I want nothing more than to be free of them. The walls close in on me, making my heart pound in my ears. I strain my eyes toward the commotion, worried for Seung.

Another omega, pushed around by the same male as I was, cries as he straps her to the bench next to me.

"Seung!"

I call for him. The woman beside me cries harder.

"Seung! Answer me! Seung! Please be okay!"

"Shut up, bitch."

My ears ring from the handler's backhand, his arm long enough to reach me even as he ties down another woman.

The sky lightens with every breath, but no matter how hard I lean against my bindings, I can't find the only person I know in the galaxy.

Despite the fiery throbbing of my cheek, I look up into the reflective face mask and plead with every ounce of desperation I have.

"Please! He's the father of my child."

The large male frame blocks the opening. His silhouette fills me with dread as he swivels his head to look over his shoulder at me.

"You're going to regret saying that."

He jumps from the tailgate and speaks words I can't hear through the sobs of the women around me.

Seung's limp frame, dangling between two white-clothed brutes, crosses to the other side of the vehicle. They toss him into a second transporter before turning and disappearing back into the wreckage.

A deafening pop causes everyone to duck and scream, our bound hands straining to cover our ears despite the futility of the action—our wrists hang just out of reach of our right ear. Agony digs into my thighs as the flesh between my leg bands and the seat strap gets pinched between the two unrelenting bindings. After several long, confusing moments, I grit my teeth and train my blurry eyes out the open tailgate, surprised to see the flames of my wrecked cruise ship in the distance.

We're moving?

Light pink sky with faint blue streaks of sunlight fills the open space. Weightlessness tightens my stomach as the transporter hurtles through the air before it plummets toward the ground.

Chaos. Screaming. Pain.

Seung's limp body flashes through my mind's eye.

The engine whines louder as it charges up a hill, revealing the massive mounds of sand that make up the landscape. Startled at the bleak barrenness of the climate, I turn frantic eyes to my more immediate surroundings.

Seven other women sit strapped to the vehicle while two alphas in white suits stand holding onto handles on the roof. Even with the mask shielding his face, I feel the closest one eyeing me, his interest lingering on the swell of my belly.

Bile rises up my throat. I swallow it down too late, the sour taste hitting the back of my tongue and making my situation worse.

Something heavy lands on the roof.

The two alphas curse and pull weapons from their belts. Words pass between them, and after a few odd pauses, I realize they wear communicators and speak with other people.

Their actions don't make sense to me, but they move with such speed and grace I know they've practiced them before. One yanks a tiny black thing from his belt while the other grabs a lever on the ceiling near the front of the vehicle. Half a second later, the black disc disappears through a tiny porthole before the alpha uses the lever to close the hole back up.

My ears ring as an explosion detonates over my head.

More silent than death, too big for the cramped space, a dark shape slinks in through the back opening. Blood sprays over white cloth as a knife pierces the furthest alpha's throat. Before he even hits the ground, the goliath form rips the mask off the other alpha's head and buries a blade into his eye socket.

I lean forward and lose the contents of my stomach.

My head spins when I try to lift it, so I let it hang while I struggle to regain my senses.

Soft fabric presses against my lips. I jerk away, knocking my temple against the elbow of the woman beside me.

A pathetic whimper leaves my throat as I freeze in shock. I must have hit my head too hard. The monster standing in front of me can't be real.

With shoulders twice as wide as the alphas lying dead on the floor, eyes a brighter blue than the sky at midday, and covered from head to toe in black, the creature keeps his hand extended for a moment before dropping the square of cloth onto my lap.

When he leans forward, I flinch and wish I could curl into myself and protect my protruding belly.

Sky blue irises pierce mine.

"I'm not going to hurt you, tiny mama. I'm here to protect you."

I blink and wish I'd let him wipe my mouth instead of overreacting. Weird, inexplicable things happen deep within my heart, the neglected organ giving a sluggish thump.

Those eyes do not belong to a human. The shape seems off, yet so right. I could drown in them and never have another care ever again.

His hand moves closer. Digits easily four times bigger than mine reach toward my face.

I can't help my flinch, nor the shaking of my bones.

"Be still. Let me untie you, then you can help release the others. Yes?"

My lips move despite the tingling numbness spreading throughout my body.

"Yes, please. I want to help."

"Ah, a polite little mama."

He closes the distance between our hands. When his glove ghosts across my wrist, a broken piece of me wishes he wasn't wearing them so we could touch flesh to flesh.

The moment the pressure releases from my wrists, I hiss and try to lift them, but the stranger cups them in his mighty palm and lowers them carefully to my lap.

"Take it slow. Let me—"

"Get them all untied. Now. Sky-Flyer inbound."

All chins except for *his* snap toward the newcomer. Larger than the human alphas, but not as massive as the male in front of me, the new monster crouches to reach the first omega on the bench. His broad shoulders boast irregularly shaped plates that fit together like a puzzle and look thicker than my wrist.

No wonder his suit leaves his shoulders and back bare—he has built-in armor.

He releases my fellow captors with quick motions, ignoring the terrified expressions aimed at him.

The massive alpha unhooks the strap around my lap and shifts his attention to the woman beside me. I bite back the urge to snarl, battling shock at the knee-jerk reaction.

I've only snarled once in my life—during my first and only heat, when common sense melted away and left nothing but needy instincts behind.

My emotions careen around uncontrollably. I have no reason to insult such a powerful, terrifying beast with a snarl, especially since I'm in such a vulnerable position.

After rubbing my wrists and flexing my fingers to hurry my circulation, I grit my teeth and focus on the female directly across from me.

Dark eyes and matted hair top familiar features, and I flick my gaze around, desperate to see her little boy nearby, but her sharp cry yanks my attention back to her face.

"Help me!"

I brace my palms on the bench and force my legs to accept my weight, intending to shuffle across the space and unbind her. Halfway up, the floor shifts under me as the vehicle crests another dune. As clumsy as ever, I teeter sideways, knocking into muscles so hard I may as well have hit a brick wall.

Massive digits close around my bicep.

"Sit down."

I can't. Despite how my legs shake and my heart threatens to burst from my chest, I'll never be able to forgive myself if I don't help.

"I'm okay. Get them free."

He pushes me back into a seated position. As soon as he releases me, I lunge across the cargo bay and catch myself by bracing my palms on either side of the other mother's legs.

"Sorry. S-sorry, I'm trying."

"Hurry. My wrists."

I tear at the restraints until I find the release. By the time I get her hands free, all but her and one other omega are completely free of their binds, the large alphas quick to release the others.

With urgency flowing through me, I unhook the band around her thighs and step sideways to the last bound woman.

The vehicle bounces and swerves, sending me too far. Yet again, I slam into hard muscles.

"Sit down. You're too slow."

As he pushes me onto the bench by my shoulders, hurt flows through me at his terse words. Clear blue eyes meet mine.

Cold one second and yet too soft the next, he releases my shoulders and unstraps the woman as he speaks.

"I'm sorry, little mama. I didn't mean to be so rude."

Words clog my throat.

How can someone so big show such gentleness?

"Hayden, baby, come here," the woman beside me sobs as she leans forward. Tiny shoulders emerge from under the bench, her little boy hidden away behind her skirts.

My relief bursts from my chest on a ragged cry. I slap both hands over my mouth and let my tears slip from my eyes.

"My brave little boy. You listened so well. It's ok, cry now. I have you."

Instinctively, my palms caress my waistline, seeking confirmation of my baby's survival as I watch the other mother cradle her son in her lap. He clings to her and cries the tears of an innocent, so terrified and yet so brave.

A deep, scratchy voice fills the cargo bay, the sound so menacing we fall silent the second it begins.

"You don't know us and we don't know you, but we're your only hope for survival."

The owner of the voice, a third larger-than-life figure, leans into the back of the vehicle, half of his body out of sight since he clings to the side of the craft. His white pupils and black irises are unlike anything I've ever seen and fill me with instinctual dread.

"If you listen to us, we'll get you somewhere safe. There's no time to explain further. Jump and roll. Stay where you land. We will not leave the area until we have a proper head count."

He doesn't even glance to see if we understand. My head reels.

He wants us to jump from a moving vehicle? What if I can't? What if I get hurt or land wrong and hurt my baby?

How can he ask the mother sitting next to me to do such a thing? She has a young child in her arms.

"Thret, lead the way," says the alpha clinging to the outside of the vehicle.

Instead of jumping from the tailgate, the bony plated monster turns and scoops the woman and child off the bench beside me.

My lungs seize as he drops out of sight without so much as a single word of comfort for the delicate beings in his arms.

I consider refusing to jump but know I can't. After what happened in here, there's no way I can stay. Whoever wears the white suits don't have my well-being in mind.

But these alphas wearing black... can I really trust them?

I rise onto shaky legs as my mind races through improbable options, my brain searching for a way out of this predicament. As the crowd in front of me shuffles closer to the door, I know I can't do it. Even with the dead bodies lying on the floor, I won't be able to force myself to jump.

With only two more omegas left before it's my turn, the transporter hits a dip in the sand and bounces so hard my feet leave the floor. I squeak and try to keep upright, hoping beyond hope to land on my feet for once, but prepare to land on my butt, like always. My frazzled mind watches as the lady in front of me lands in a crouch while I keep falling.

Gigantic arms swoop under me and lift me into the air.

Shocked at how easily he caught me, I stare up into mesmerizing blue eyes until he looks away. Embarrassment heats my cheeks as my insides flip in reaction to his closeness. My back and legs pulse with heat where his arms cradle me.

Even though I can't smell him or see any of his features besides his light blue eyes, my body comes to life as something unravels within my ribcage.

"Tuck your chin to your chest."

His voice vibrates along my side and sends a shiver up my spine.

A massive hand wraps around the back of my skull and guides my head downward.

Only when the sun hits my exposed arms and weightlessness tightens my stomach do I realize he jumped from the vehicle with me in his arms. I blink and tense for a rough landing but turn wide eyes up at his covered face when I feel nothing except his even stride as he runs toward the closest omega.

"Can you stand? Walk?"

Dazed and overwhelmed, I nod and ignore the pulsing of my body as he sets me down next to the other omega. Three others join us before I realize my eyes continue to stare at my unexpected savior as he ushers us toward the rest of our group.

His bulky frame moves through the sand with ease, a thick, tapered tail protruding from above the glorious globes of his ass. It trails behind him, not quite long enough to drag in the sand, occasionally bending and hinting at the strength held within.

I can't take my eyes off him.

What is wrong with me?

Chapter Four

Cahress

Two alphas, eight omegas, and one human boy stand in the middle of the desert. The vehicle we just vacated launches over a nearby dune, heading toward the sun as Commander Ru'en slips back into the driver's seat. His voice rumbles in my ear as he speaks to Choku and Jokur, who were chasing a second transporter, then gives curt directions to Thret and I.

As the Sky-Flyer bursts over the mountains to the west, where we were before the crash, we turn our little group north and slide down a dune to hide in the valley.

When the tiny pregnant female wobbles and almost somersaults down the slope, I reach for her. She fixes her balance before I touch her, so I pull my hand back and force myself to help a different female instead.

She calls to me without saying a word. Her deep brown eyes and delicate features affect me as much as the swell of her belly does. My protective instinct always magnifies near females, but this little one has them in overdrive. It almost hurts to watch her struggle in the deep sand.

The urge to rip my mask from my face and scent her nearly overrides my common sense, but the sound of gunfire stays my hand.

Commander Ru'en drives the transporter away, leading the Sky-Flyer on a merry chase, becoming a decoy so we can get the victims to relative safety.

When the sounds of engines fade far enough away, Thret gestures for me to round up our tiny flock. I sigh and make a crude gesture back at him, letting him know I think he's a sorry sack of shit, in the most respectful way, of course.

His eyes narrow within his mask before he shakes his head and crosses his arms over his wide chest, displaying his obstinacy.

The big boy will have to learn to speak to females one day, but obviously today is not that day.

I meet frightened faces and soften my stance.

"My name is Cahress and that ugly mug over there is Thret. We're headed northeast toward the mountains. Stay together. If we don't find shelter from the sun before midday, we won't survive. If you need help, call out. We'll do what we can to keep you moving—no one will be left behind."

After perusing the sooty, battered humans in front of me, I decide to include another tactic.

"I'm going to pair you up with at least one other female. Help each other, but still don't hesitate to call out. Understand?"

Already huddled together, the omegas don't balk as I assign couples. Most link arms together, their natural instincts seeking close company in their time of need. Social creatures at heart, omegas need someone else to nurture, as well as emotional support when things get too difficult.

I pair them according to their stance and expression—putting a timid, younger female with an older, stern looking woman. Two of the taller omegas loop their arms together, one blinking as though she can't remember how she got here while the other trains her gaze toward our destination.

I put the mother and son with the female who jumped from the vehicle first, her body practically vibrating with her need to keep moving. She exudes nervous energy, but her deep breaths and clear eyes lead me to believe she'll have no problem carrying the boy when his mother gets tired. Thret dips his chin in acknowledgement when I signal for him to keep the boy at the front of the pack.

He grunts a word and sets off around the dune, picking out the easiest route even though it means a longer trek.

The little mama and her travel companion, one of the other shorter omegas, weave their fingers together and follow the second set of omegas, leaving another couple between myself and her.

Looking over their heads as they set off, I realize the pregnant female may be the youngest in our group, besides the boy. She couldn't have been through more than two or three heats, and her tiny frame seems too petite to carry the burden of new life.

My thoughts do nothing but rile my insane urge to snatch her up and hold her in my arms.

The sun rises higher into the cloudless sky until the sand sizzles under my boots. I check our back trail often, staying vigilant despite the vast emptiness of the desert. A hot, dry wind kicks up clouds of sand, prompting the women to do whatever they can to cover their faces. My heart shoots into my throat and I almost dart around the couple in front of me to grab the little mama, but I swallow the irrational panic when I realize she's crouching to pull at the hem of her skirt, not because she fell.

I stalk to her.

"What are you doing?"

Rich brown eyes squint up at me. I shift to put her in my shadow to alleviate her eye strain.

"I want to use a strip from the bottom of my skirt as a face covering, but it won't—"

She gasps as I squat and slice about four inches off her skirt, my knife sliding free of its holster and cutting the fabric with ease. Before she reacts further, I pull her to a standing position and place the strip of material in her hand and step backward.

Her naturally pale face sports a bruise on her right cheek and red splotches from the sand and sun, but she doesn't move to cover it. In a dazzling display of resilience, she gathers herself and speaks.

"Thank you, Cahress."

I nod and force myself to stand still. The need to hold her in my arms grows with each passing second, but she turns away and fashions a head wrap on her omega partner.

Too stunned at her actions, I stand like a brain-dead fool as she weaves the fabric over the woman's head, face, and shoulders.

With a start, I realize her partner wears shorts and a shirt too low-cut to pull up and cover her face. This tiny mama is too sweet and nurturing for her own good. Now, every step she takes exposes the creamy flesh of her ankles and shins, leaving them at the mercy of the elements.

When the last couple walks around me and follows their fellow survivors, I shake myself out of my trance and close the distance I shouldn't have allowed to come between the parties.

Only myself and Thret walk with sure footing. The sun beats down on everything in sight, and even though the mountains seem to loom over us, I know we still have at least two miles before we reach the base of the range.

My sweet little mama teeters again, making every muscle in my body tense, but her partner pulls her upright. She takes two more steps before her heel slides out from under her.

I dart forward and catch her shoulders with my forearms, catching her head in the crook of my right elbow. Even with her eyes glazed, she stuns me with her beauty as she tries to focus on my face.

"You're upside down."

Her voice sounds so dry and brittle my own throat aches in response. I look beyond her sunburn and bruises and notice a pallor that wasn't there before and almost curse out loud.

At a loss for the first time in a long while, I swallow a wave of emotion and ease her the last few inches down onto the sand.

"You're upside down, too," I murmur as I slip the long tube connected to my water pouch free of its clip.

"Here, little mama. Take a few sips, then I'll carry you."

Her brows pinch and lips purse.

"I'm fine, thank you."

"No, you aren't. You pushed too hard."

The urge to bend down and brush my nose against hers as she scrunches her dainty features has me drifting closer to her, but my mask reminds me to mind my distance.

Her partner drops to her knees beside her.

"Duri, drink the water. You're not okay."

I look from the kneeling woman to the little mama as awe sends chills up and down my spine. Locking Duri's name into my memory, I can't help but let my lips tilt up in a small smile, knowing my eyes will reflect my emotions but unable to curb the reverence I feel toward her.

In the few grueling hours since we began our trek, my little mama earned this woman's trust and loyalty. Instead of snatching the hose from my hand or demanding a drink for herself, the woman urges Duri to take a few sips.

"What abou—"

I shove the mouthpiece between her teeth before they close and squeeze water through the hose, forcing her to either swallow or waste the precious resource.

Confused brown eyes meet mine before she consumes the trickle of life sustaining water. Her body realizes what I offer and begins gulping down the tepid liquid. After three swallows, I pry her teeth apart and take away the mouthpiece.

"C'mon, up you go."

As I scoop her up and stand to my full height, she stares at my face as emotions play over her features.

"More?"

Her request almost guides my hand to offer her the water straw again, but I shake my head and lean so her partner can use my elbow as leverage to stand.

"Not yet, little mama. We must save it for when we find shade."

"Why?"

"I'll show you when we get there. For now, trust me."

She surprises me by sighing and relaxing into my arms, her cheek pressing against my pectoral. When her friend releases my elbow and shuffles forward, I make a sound of disapproval and take a step so we're even.

"I'll carry her. You hold on to me. Almost there."

Despite the wariness lurking in her tired eyes, the omega nods and slips her fingers into the crook of my elbow, wedging them between my arm and Duri's legs.

A few steps later and the little mama goes completely lax. My steps falter as her left hand slides off her belly and drops to hang in the air.

"Shit!"

A terror more potent than anything I've felt since the ISC targeted my home world and nearly murdered my family seizes my lungs. I lift my omega's limp body and press my ear against her chest.

Her heart, though strained, thumps out a steady rhythm. I breathe a sigh of relief and continue walking, meeting her friend's worried gaze.

"She pushed herself too hard, the crazy little female, but she'll be fine once we get out of this heat."

The omega nods and ducks her head to focus on her feet. A mile trek is nothing to me, but these poor souls struggle with every step. I check the duo behind us and shorten my strides to give them a chance to catch up.

The woman beside me reaches up and puts my little mama's hand back on the swell of her abdomen, giving the limp digits a quick caress to ensure herself my omega is okay.

I berate myself. When did I start thinking of this tiny female as my own?

She can't be mine. Considering her delicate condition, she must already be marked and claimed. If I were to take my mask off, surely her scent would confirm her unavailability and erase whatever ridiculous infatuation I harbor for her. I need to ignore whatever pulls me toward her. Need to get her somewhere safe and walk away. Need to stop dreaming about keeping her.

Except, I can't bring myself to take off my mask. Even if it's just for a little while, and complete folly, I want to imagine a world where this tiny, fragile omega is mine to protect and cherish. I want to pretend like the child in her womb belongs to me. I want to hold her close and learn everything there is to know about her.

I want her.

My heart beats faster as I admit the truth to myself.

She can't be mine, but I want her.

What if her mate died in the crash?

I should be skewered alive for my joyous response to her alpha's potential death. As penance, I peel my eyes away from her face and focus on the mountains ahead.

I keep torturing myself, not allowing myself even a glimpse of her form as we near the mountains.

Chapter Five

Duri

Coolness seeps in through the burning of my flesh, slowly waking me until my eyelids agree to lift. Nothing makes sense for a moment, the odd shapes clinging to the ceiling confusing me until I realize I stare at the roof of a cave. I turn my head and see nothing but drab gray surfaces and faint light glimmering off speckled minerals.

Swinging my attention in the other direction, I suck in a startled sound as I meet eyes so reflective they seem white instead of light blue.

"Where—"

"Oh, thank the gods you're awake." Henna, the woman who kept me sturdy through the most strenuous moments of my life, lays her hand on mine and speaks in a rush. "I thought you wouldn't want to wake up in the dark, so I asked him to wait here until you woke."

I blink at her sunburnt face until my neck aches. Another blink later and I finally realize why the angle is so odd—I'm still cradled in the alpha's arms, so the top of her head barely reaches my hip.

My stomach does a weird somersault. In response, the new life in my womb jerks and kicks.

Relief sweeps through me, but sandpaper scratches the back of my eyes instead of tears.

"C'mon, little females. Let's get you the water your bodies so desperately need."

The world spins as he turns to move further away from the faint sunlight.

"Thank you, but I can walk."

My hoarse voice does not imbue confidence, but the alpha stops and lowers my feet to the ground. His movements hold a reluctance I feel in my marrow, but it doesn't seem fair for him to carry me when everyone else walks.

I lift my foot to take a step and flail as my toe catches on a rock. Before I fall too far forward, massive arms wrap around me and haul me upward.

With one arm under my belly and the other across my shoulders, the massive brute plasters my back against his front.

Before I can decide if my ears are faulty or if he makes a strained sound, his rumbly voice destroys my concentration.

"I'll carry you, since you can't seem to put one foot in front of the other without performing a gravity check."

Even with the humor tinting his voice, his suggestion of my natural aptitude for accidents embarrasses me more than I care to admit.

"I just couldn't see anything. I'll be fine to walk."

Warm fabric rubs against the top of my head, and I shake as I realize he ghosts his covered lips across my hair in an unexpectedly intimate caress.

"You're trembling."

My bones try to melt into goo, but I swallow so hard the pain in my throat keeps me tense.

"I can still w—"

"After you get some food, water, and rest. Don't argue, little mama, or I might decide to never set you down."

Stunned at how easily he declares such a monumental statement, I don't fight when he shifts me around until I lay cradled in his arms again.

It feels right.

My shaking worsens as the realization sinks into my mind. The buzz of worry and fear I've carried in my chest my entire life eases when I'm in his arms. Even in our dire circumstances, something behind my sternum reaches toward him, yearning for things I don't have words for.

As the darkness thickens around us, my ears pick up Henna's footsteps, my hearing heightening to make up for the loss of my vision. Even knowing I can't make out his features, I train my gaze toward his face, struggling with my ridiculous thoughts.

My jaw aches as I grit my teeth.

His footsteps make no sound, whereas I know exactly where Henna is because of her shoes clacking on stone.

A bubble of light reveals a group of omegas huddled together, everyone except the other alpha within the circle of lamplight. The soft yellow light illuminates the wall of rock behind them but doesn't carry across the oblong cave. I shift my gaze upward and fight unease—ominous darkness looms over us, the roof of the cave too high to see.

Henna pats my shin as she steps around us and drops beside an older omega who immediately passes a water bag to her.

The woman looks up and up at my alpha. A tight ball of ugly motions condenses in my stomach. If it weren't for my thirst threatening to launch me toward the water bag, the urge to gouge out the woman's eyes might prove to be too much.

I chastise myself like the hormonal, frazzled imbecile I am. No matter how much my instincts clamor to get closer to him, he isn't mine. I know next to nothing about him, including what he looks like. His suit hides everything except the bridge of his nose and his eyes. He might even be mated already and I don't know it because his suit blocks his scent.

My subconscious must be just as rattled as my nerves are. Who wouldn't be so confused after what I've been through? I lived through a crash landing on an unknown planet. I watched my best friend—

Horror steals my breath and whisks me back to the moment when I saw Seung's limp body hanging between two white-clad forms. Adrenaline floods my system and wrecks whatever calm lingers within my heart.

Great, big, ugly sobs wrack my chest, but no tears slide down my face. No sweat slicks my skin. My dry lip cracks and bleeds, the warm liquid smearing as I cover my face with my hands.

The most magnificent sound infiltrates my ears and vibrates against my side. It permeates through my entire body, infecting every nerve ending and turning my bones to mush. The erratic beating of my heart slows into a monotonous, steady rhythm. Peace wraps around me.

I push against the hard, warm chest under my cheek, guilt breaking me from the spell of his purr, and fight to escape the cocoon of his arms.

"Stop, Duri. Calm down."

My name spoken in his rich vibrato only sends me deeper into despair.

How could I forget about Seung? How could I block out the terror of that moment? What kind of person leaves their best friend in such a horrible situation and thinks of nothing but their own survival?

"Little mama, think of your offspring. Calm yourself and drink some water."

The gentle purr underlying his words almost sends me into worse panic, but I latch on to his message and curl into as much of a ball as his arms will allow, needing to protect my baby.

With herculean effort, I gather my chaotic emotions and stomp them into the recesses of my heart, only berating myself for half a second for being such a terrible human for not only forgetting my best friend, but also not putting all my focus on the delicate life within my womb. Nothing matters more than keeping my baby alive.

Not even Seung, even though my chest aches at the thought.

And especially not this weird attraction to an alpha I know nothing about.

"Th-thank you."

A hiccup ruins my attempt to sound strong, but I take the mouthpiece from his fingers, startled anew at how thick his digits are—three of my thumbs could fit inside the circumference of his pointer finger—and stick the straw between my teeth.

The first drop of water nearly sends me into a frenzy, my thirst so overwhelming every cell in my body screams for more, but a gentle vibration and quiet murmur urge me to drink small, regulated sips.

When my stomach tightens without warning, I dart my eyes up to the alpha holding me and fling the straw toward him as I clap my palm over my mouth.

"Breathe through your nose, deep and even, and rest your head on my chest."

I want to do as he suggests, but my nausea grows and the thought of vomiting all over him upsets me almost as much as wasting the precious resource does. But when I shake my head to refuse, he cups an enormous hand over the side of my head and eases my ear to his pectoral.

His purr loosens the knots from my abdomen. The urge to purge dissipates much slower than it rose, but I pull in a shaky breath of relief and relax against him.

Exhaustion rises as my body eagerly soaks up both his comfort and the water. Unable to explain why I need to stay awake, knowing that if I start thinking about where we are or why we ended up here, my mind latches onto the most insane topic.

"Why did we have to wait to drink the water?"

A slight hitch in his purr makes me aware of our surroundings, even as my mind stamps the flash of surprise playing across the small expanse of flesh revealed by his suit into my memory bank. The lamplight barely reaches his face, since he sits a few feet away from the group of omegas.

"I did tell you I'd show you, didn't I? Just relax, little mama, and I will."

He settles me deeper into his lap and pulls his right arm out from under my knees. I blink in confusion as he pulls a small square of fabric from his pocket and dribbles water on it. A flush heats my cheeks, or maybe my skin cooks from the sunburn, but embarrassment and shame grow in my chest as he wipes the blood from my split lip off the mouthpiece.

My heart stops as he gently wipes the dried blood from my chin and bottom lip.

Another kind of heat builds in my veins, echoing the appreciation shining from his eyes as he studies my lips. My clit pulses, reminding me of the incessant ache I've suffered since my hormones kicked up after my first trimester.

This won't do. If I slick too much, the artificial plug holding Seung's seed inside my womb will dissolve much too fast. It usually lasts two or three days, but with the tragic events over the last few hours, I might lose it early.

The thought terrifies me.

I push his hand aside and scramble to search my pockets. The swell of my belly makes it difficult to twist, but after a few seconds of squirming, I find the bottle of pills and pull it from my pocket.

A half sob, half sigh escapes my chest.

I lift the bottle up to the light and count how many are left. A sting of pain reminds me not to chew on my injured lip.

If the ship hadn't crashed, I would have refilled my prescription before I left the medical room, but I didn't get a chance. Only six capsules rattle around the bottom of the bottle.

"What are those?"

Swallowing my emotions, knowing I'll cry if I open my mouth, I rotate the bottle until the label faces him.

A moment later, he stiffens.

The movement rubs his gigantic cock along my bottom, the thin layers of fabric between our bodies doing nothing to hide his engorged state.

I freeze in shock.

Common sense, or maybe fear or guilt, launches me from his lap. Rock bruises my body as I roll away from him. I finish on my hands and knees and scramble to crawl away.

Mended and Marked

Gloved digits wrap around my left ankle.

Chapter Six

Cahress

I shouldn't grab her, but her retreat kickstarts my feral instincts to catch and claim.

After filling my lungs and expelling the trapped air on a slow breath, I release her ankle, both surprised and relieved when she doesn't move after I let her go. She turns frightened eyes over her shoulder at me, wary confusion filling her expression.

"Sorry, little mama. It was a reflex, nothing more. I won't hurt you."

"But, you're—" her eyes flick downward before she yanks them back to my face, "You, um… you won't…"

"I've never hurt an omega before, and I don't plan to start now. My mother would skin me alive."

"Your mother would do what?"

"It's an expression. She'd make my life miserable."

"Oh... Where is your mother?"

The tremor in her voice sends electricity through my veins. I want her to shake when I touch her, but not because she's scared.

I want her trembling and needy under me, so ready for my cock she can't help but beg. For the first time since adolescence, my control nearly fails me. I ignore the lifting of my ruff as electricity tingles up and down my spine, glad when my suit limits the thick fluff from expanding. The pinching discomfort, along with the abrasive material of my underpants on my hard cock, distracts me enough to keep me in the moment.

"My mother pilots the second largest craft in our fleet, so she's in orbit."

"Really? In orbit of this planet?"

Her eyes look everywhere but at me. Strain tightens her expression.

I sigh and dig my fingers into my thighs to stop myself from pulling her back into my lap.

"Duri, this position hurts you. Either come back to the comfort of my arms or join the others."

Her pupils shrink and shoulders tighten, but she doesn't move. Confusion creases her brow as she stares directly into my soul.

"You won't hurt me, no matter my choice?"

"I won't."

A few agonizing heartbeats later, she sits back on her heels and braces her palm on the cave floor. I swallow my disappointment as she tries to stand.

Her gasp of pain pulls me forward. I grab her hand as she lifts it from the jagged stone, irrational fury demanding I rage at the piece of rock and pulverize it to dust as I turn her hand over. Dark liquid wells up from two new puncture marks on her palm.

Before she reacts, I unzip a pocket on my vest and yank out a sterilized packet of medicated gauze. Ripping open the plastic with my teeth, I wrap her hand, ensuring the ointment covers the new wounds, before using my thumb to apply pressure.

The visual of her delicate palm engulfed by my much bigger thumb makes me pause.

Very few sentient beings are larger than I, but the sheer size difference between us seems insurmountable.

It's probably for the best she's already claimed.

I bury my disappointment and help her to her feet.

The ease with which I forget her pregnancy concerns me for less than a second before my basal needs demand I care for her. I guide her to the group of omegas and help her sit, glaring at the cold, uneven stone for being so unforgiving, and place the water bag beside her before stepping out of the circle of light.

Thret appears at my side, the shape of his bony plates so similar to the surrounding stone I struggle to pick out his form despite my acute vision. When he scowls and taps his earpiece, I reach up and swap mine to a lower frequency.

After a few moments, I nod and watch as Thret disappears toward the exit, waiting for the full coded message to finish before swapping back to the original frequency.

"Sir?"

One of the older females stands at the edge of the light, holding an almost empty water bag.

Knowing she can't see my lips, but hoping the shift in my eyes will ease her, I smile and step forward just far enough so she can pass me the water bag.

"Did Thret explain how the processor works, or did he just snarl at you to leave some water in the bag?"

Although still huddled together, suffering through a mixture of shock and exhaustion, many of the females lose the terrified edge in their posture at my rueful tone.

"He didn't explain anything."

"Wonderful. I love teaching, especially when I already have a captivated audience."

The woman standing in front of me huffs out a half laugh before limping back to her spot and sitting down. As I fish the high-tech processor out of the hidden pocket along my tricep, I unscrew the mouthpiece from the straw with my thumb and pointer finger.

Light brown eyes steal my attention, the flash of jealousy flitting across my little mama's face filling me with satisfaction. She blinks and seems to shake herself, offering the straw to the woman beside her.

I hide my pleasure and ignore my throbbing cock as I drop into a squat beside her. Despite my nearness, none of the omegas shy away. Lines of exhaustion show on their sunburnt and wind chapped faces, and without thinking about it, I gentle my voice as I talk through my actions.

Even though I can't take their pain and worry away, I can distract them from it for a few minutes.

Memories resurface as I push the oddly shaped processor into a sand-filled crevice between the stones of the floor. I use the same teaching cadence as I did for my sisters when I was younger. Bittersweet emotions rise, but I keep them tamped down as I use words simple enough for frazzled minds to grasp.

My sisters' bright, eager eyes and mischievous smiles always filled me with pride and taught me to treasure the unexpected strength hidden within the feminine gender.

Fitting the end of the straw to the uneven surface of the processor, I squeeze a few drops of water toward the end of the hose and press the button on top before continuing my explanation.

"People much smarter than I built this nifty little processor. Basically, it takes whatever substance you feed into it on this side—" I point to the droplet of water leaking from the hose and trace a path halfway around the circumference of the device, following an almost nonsensical line between the minuscule indents as I explain "—and it pulls it through a molecular analysis. When it reaches right about here—" I tap the midpoint and continue a slower trail around the device "—it sucks similar elements from the compounds touching the underside. Within a few seconds, the processor uses the energy produced from the shifting molecules to seek out a more natural means of transporting the substance to the processor. After maybe another ten seconds, it channels the appropriate substance through any surface and—" I flick my eyes toward Duri's face, eager to see her expression "—finishes the circuit by multiplying the output."

As clean water rushes up the straw, light brown eyes widen in wonder, breaking the mesmerized quality of her stare. My next words emerge rough and thick as I battle a wave of desire, bewitched by both her innocent fascination and the hint of lust in her previous expression.

"As amazing as this device is, it has its faults. For example, you must already have the substance you need to find more of it."

I force myself to continue speaking, even as her appreciative eyes watch me lift the rapidly filling water sack.

"Which is why we couldn't drink during our trek. The risk of running out of water was too high, especially with a group this size. But we should be staying put for a few hours, so drink your fill now and rest while you can."

I reach over my little mama, stretching the water hose across her lap, and set the nearly full sack next to her far hip. When I lean even further, invading her space and brushing my shoulder with hers, she turns startled orbs up at me. I can't deny my smirk at her frazzled expression, but I pick up the mostly empty bag and retreat.

She pushes out a shaky exhale.

Gods, she's too fucking cute.

I bend down further than necessary, pinching my wayward cock in retribution for its persistence, and swap out the straws before the first one overflows.

Once I set the second bag to refill, I sneak a glance at the face I'll never forget and nearly curse aloud. Guilt shines plain as day on her face and her shoulders slump forward as though defeat weighs heavily on them.

Shit. I shouldn't tease her. She's in no state for flirting.

I plaster her unhappy expression onto the forefront of my mind, using the ache it causes in my chest to curb my natural urges.

She's not mine and can never be mine.

The knowledge hurts, but I turn it into my litany, repeating it over and over in my mind to solidify the facts. Hopefully, with time, my stubborn soul will stop yearning after an omega I can never have.

Using more care than necessary, I turn off the processor and pop the mouthpiece back onto the straw before offering it to my—*not mine*—little mama. She shakes her head and pushes it away without looking up.

Utter stillness overtakes the cave, skyrocketing my senses to high alert, the sudden tension within the group of females grating on my nerves. I freeze and place the water bag on the floor, fighting shame and aggravation as I realize the root cause of their terror.

Me.

My snarl still echoes off stone.

"Take the water, little mama."

Ashen underneath her bruised and abraded face, Duri finally lifts her head and meets my gaze. What she sees there, I don't know, but she surprises me by straightening her shoulders and spreading her hands over the top of her belly.

"I didn't mean to offend you. Thank you, but I—" her voice falters, but she forges onward, "I just had the other water sack. This one should go to someone else."

The urge to help her as she struggles to her feet nearly wins, but I remain seated by sheer force of will as she shuffles around me and places the bag between the two omegas on my left. When she returns to her spot but blinks at the ground instead of lowering herself down, my body moves of its own will. I twist and offer her my upturned palms, unable to turn my gaze away as emotions flit across her features. After a few moments of debate, she grips my gloved hands and uses me for balance, settling onto her rump and crossing her legs before releasing me.

"Thank you."

I bite back the praise my tongue so eagerly wants to speak, nodding and standing instead.

Such a polite little mama shouldn't have to put up with an overbearing, war hardened alpha such as myself.

After I turn and slink into the darkness, the omegas relax, many of them gathering closer together and laying down despite the cool, unforgiving cave floor. My little mama—no, *Duri*, I must call her by her name, not by what my heart wants to call her—stays sitting for a few minutes longer, swallowing a pill from her coveted bottle and exchanging a few words with the mother and boy before lowering herself onto her side.

I turn around and close my eyes. Pain lances through my chest, the visual of her curves backlit by the lamp embedding into my soul and overriding every effort I've made to distance myself from her.

I can't. I can't have her. I shouldn't want her. I should back away and let my teammates ensure her comfort and survival.

But I know I won't. I want her.

My hands clench into fists as I imagine Thret or Ru'en caring for her. Touching her. Hearing her voice. Carrying her. Seeing her sweet smile.

No. For the same reason I haven't taken off my mask to scent her, I won't step away: I don't want this to end.

Even though we're doomed to go our separate ways, I don't want our time together to end so abruptly. I don't want this pull in my chest to go away.

I don't want distance between us.

If that makes me a cold, selfish bastard, then so be it.

Chapter Seven

Duri

Exhaustion pulls me into sleep so quickly I don't feel the hard stone bruising my hip and shoulder until I jolt awake. Disoriented in the low lamplight, I lie still until my brain catches up to my predicament. Clutching the pill bottle in my right hand and feeling tiny limbs beating against the splayed palm of my left, I search for why I woke so suddenly and nearly groan when I shift. My bladder complains of fullness.

It's a good sign, but not a pleasant sensation. As quietly as I can, but not bothering to be graceful since every part of me hurts, I fight against gravity and force my body to a sitting position.

"What's wrong?"

The low, rough voice emerges from the darkness and nearly yanks a scream from my throat. Pills rattle against plastic as I thunk the bottle against my racing heart. A few shaky breaths later and my fright dissolves.

"I, um…"

Embarrassment has no place here, and yet a blush heats my cheeks. I shift my weight and bite back a groan of discomfort, using the urgent need to push past my social hang-ups.

"I need to relieve myself."

Broad shoulders emerge from the darkness, Cahress' black suit seeming to erase whatever light touches it, creating a pitch-black silhouette against the yellow light reflecting off the cave walls.

"C'mon then, little mama, I'll help you up."

A massive arm extends and offers me intimidatingly huge digits. Remembering his gentle touch as he bandaged my palm, I accept his offer with trembling fingers.

He lifts me as though I'm as light as a feather, but the controlled power vibrating through his form assures me he won't hurt me. My legs shake and my spine complains as my weight settles on my sore feet.

Two grueling steps later and the ground disappears. I tighten my grip on the pill bottle and instinctively wrap an arm over my belly, but firm muscles suspend me several feet above the floor.

My gasp echoes in my ears, but I close my mouth and pull air in through my nose. By the time my breathing settles enough to speak, his steady strides carry me away from the sleeping omegas.

"Can you warn me next time?"

"What would be the fun in that?"

"Fun?"

"Yes, fun. I enjoy your cute little sounds."

Shock glues my tongue to the roof of my mouth for a moment before I regain my senses.

"It frightens me. I always expect the worst."

His footsteps pause, but he continues down the narrow passage before he speaks.

"Why?"

"Why what?"

"Why do you always expect the worst?"

"Because I'm not the most coordinated person in the best of times, and right now, when it matters the most, my balance is the worst."

My palm caresses my expanding abdomen, a wave of sadness knocking into me from nowhere. I fight back unexpected tears.

Darn these hormones.

The world shifts as gigantic arms lower me to my feet. He pivots me to face him with hands so gentle a tear escapes my lashes. A gloved digit wipes it away, startling me in the darkness. Besides a small streak of light sneaking in through a crack in the ceiling, the world seems cloaked in pitch black.

How can he see my tears when I can barely decipher where his silhouette stands?

"I can't promise not to scoop you up whenever I please, but I can promise to protect you. So, until we get to base camp, let go of your fears. Trust me enough to see both you and your offspring to safety."

My heart gives a prolonged squeeze as sincerity flows from his every word. The lump in my throat grows, but I force it lower into my chest and nod.

His thick thumb sweeps across my cheekbone again before he steps backward and disappears into the darkness.

I feel lost. Like I'm drifting in a sea of nothingness.

"I'll be back in less than five minutes."

His gentle reminder of why I'm standing alone in a cave heats my cheeks again. I wait a few moments, listening for his footsteps, but the beast moves so silently I know I wouldn't hear him even if he stomped through the passageway.

My bladder pinches a warning, so I hurry through relieving myself, tucking the bottle in my pocket, lifting my skirt, and carefully using the wall behind me for balance.

I step away, noticing the soft sand under my sandals for the first time, and drop my skirt once I'm out of the danger zone. After taking another step along the wall, a mirth filled huff leaves me. My skirt no longer reaches my ankles, since Cahress cut the bottom edge free, so my efforts to keep it dry were pointless.

"That's a cute sound, too."

I clap my hand over my mouth to stop my squeak of alarm.

He doesn't give further warning before lifting me into his arms again. The lost sensation ends as tendrils of yearning branch out from my sternum and reach for him.

"Cahress?"

His purred response tightens my lower back and I squeeze my thighs together, fearful the arousal pounding through my clit will produce too much slick.

"I..." I don't know exactly what I want to tell him, but the swirl of emotions needs an outlet before I explode, so I express myself in the only way my mind will allow. "Thank you."

"Don't thank me, Duri. It's my pleasure. After all, what alpha doesn't dream of saving a damsel in distress?"

His playful tone and unexpected words yank a half giggle from me.

"You're ridiculous."

I freeze in horror. How could I say such a thing to such a massive alpha? He isn't Seung—I haven't known him for years, nor should I ridicule him. In fact, even hinting at an insult would be the stupidest thing I could do, especially since he carries me through a pitch-black tunnel deep in a mountain.

"Be that as it may, I don't plan to change anytime soon, so get used to it, little mama."

I blink as a small smile lifts my lips, the lamplight revealing the teasing mirth shining from his eyes. He squats and sets me down in the circle of sleeping omegas, placing me on my rump as though I'm made of glass. Thick fingers sweep my long, straight hair from my face.

My heart does a somersault within my squeezed ribs, almost in time with the child rolling around in my womb.

"Get another hour or two of sleep, if you can. I'm here if you need anything."

"Thank you, Cahress."

My whisper carries no farther than his ears, creating an irrational bubble of intimacy in my mind. His eyes, so light a blue they seem yellow in the lamplight, gentle with a luminescent honesty so potent my heart skips a beat.

"Anytime, Duri."

He turns and disappears into the darkness. I settle onto my side and drift into an exhausted slumber. Inexplicable joy blooms in my soul so slowly I don't recognize it until beautiful petals color my dreams.

Despite the many dangers I face, no worries or pain reach me.

A massive, mysterious beast with shining blue eyes and a decadent voice prevents any woes from finding me. Whatever the future holds, whatever brought me to this point, nothing matters except the healing sleep my body so desperately needs.

I wake much slower than last time, small discomforts sneaking into my consciousness and pulling me from a deep pit of theoretical pillows. Before I register the movement of other omegas and the high-pitched voice of an agitated boy, I sigh in unhappiness. I don't want to leave the peace of my slumber, but tiny feet drum against my ribs and voices rise around me.

Pushing against the cool rock near my shoulder, I sit up and rub my face. My stomach gives a disgruntled rumble and sudden nausea fills my mouth with saliva. Breathing through my nose, I search for a water sack and tap Henna's shoulder when I see one sitting on her other side. When she glances at me, I request the water with a gesture as I pull the pills from my pocket.

My head spins as I twist open the container.

"Are you okay, Duri?"

I nod and take the hose from her before popping a pill in my mouth and chugging a few swallows of water.

"Just sore and tired. You?"

"Same. Hungry, too."

"Yeah, me too."

"So is the little boy, apparently. We have nothing to give him, do we?" Henna asks as Hayden's voice grows increasingly distressed.

"Unfortunately, no. We were at the end of our mission when we saw your spacecraft crash, so we weren't prepared to feed ourselves, much less others," Cahress says as he steps from the shadows and pulls the processor from his hidden pocket.

I study him as he crouches next to me with the other water sack. Before, when he explained how it worked, my brain had short-circuited with how masculine and mesmerizing his body, voice, and aura had been, but now I look past his magnetism and wonder what else he hides within his suit.

Besides his gigantic size, the shape of his eyes, and the thick, tapered tail trailing from his lower back, he looks like a bulky human, but with his suit covering him from head to toe, he could be any species.

Curiosity causes me to stare too long.

Clear blue orbs break my ruminations, the raised brow over his right eye broadcasting his amusement.

"So, what do we do now?" Henna asks, ending the charged moment.

Everyone except Hayden falls silent, turning our attention to Cahress and waiting with held breath for his response.

"Our original pickup was over seventy miles north—and five hours ago—so, base camp already knows something big enough happened to stop us from meeting the rendezvous point. And the planet's official government has already found your crash site, so we can't get picked up nearby. Plus—"

"Wait, you aren't the official government? Why are you hiding?"

The scratchy tenor voice comes from the woman sitting on the far side of Hayden's mother, the omega who walked through the desert with the mother and son duo.

"We've only been on Mai'CuS for about nine months, but we don't plan on leaving. Our fleet commander has ties to the Alpha Elites—living, breathing, walking weapons in human form created by the planet's government with the help of the local ISC branch."

"But why are you hiding from the government?"

Cahress keeps his voice calm despite the female's accusatory tone.

"The population of Mai'CuS believe they are the only life in the universe—they aren't aware extraterrestrial beings exist. Meaning even you, who look human, would be ill-treated when they realized you're technically an alien."

"What about the other passengers, the ones who were still at the crash site?"

"The fleet commander will do all she can to intercept before the local government causes them harm."

"What about us? We have no food. We can't travel. What will your fleet commander do for us?"

"Everything."

His instant and blunt response silences the entire room. The open honesty and intense belief in his tone leaves us all breathless.

What kind of leader earned this massive beast's loyalty? How can he be so sure of someone?

"Commander Minette is unlike anyone I've ever met. Add in Commander Draukir, her mate, and nothing is impossible. They've saved so many races from extinction that they shouldn't be stuck on such a sorry excuse for a planet. But this is where they've chosen to stay, so this is where we are."

A growl drifts from the entrance of the cave, freezing my blood in my veins and chilling the warmth from my bones.

Chapter Eight

Cahress

Thret scuffs his boot a few feet away, letting me know he's close, so I don't impale him on my blade.

"Relax, ladies. It's Thret, not the ISC."

"Telling love stories, Cahress?"

"It helps pass the time."

"Well, shove it up your ass and save it for later."

I raise my fist and uncurl a finger for every word he spoke until all five are raised before turning a mock startled expression toward him.

"Shit, that's the longest sentence in the history of you, isn't it? Figures it was crass, too, especially in the company of so many females."

"Shove. It."

I tamp down my roar of laughter, nearly choking on my mirth as his growl gives away his utter annoyance, resulting in a broken snort and chuckle. The sound barely bounces off the walls, but the faint echo makes me want to punch myself for being so careless.

Forcing the amusement down into my diaphragm, I sober as best as I can without giving off such a dire and deadly air as my partner—these females don't deserve to be cooped up in this dreary cave with two broody assholes.

I meet Thret's annoyed glare and respond in the most deadpan tone I can muster.

"Wait, a love story? I'm surprised you can recognize one. Little mama, pass me the water. I think Thret may be hallucinating."

Thret's expression closes further before he turns to stalk away. A few feet behind him, Commander Ru'en's white irises catch the lamplight.

"What love story?" Henna asks, her whisper directed to Duri.

"His undying devotion to Commander Minette. Careful, Cahress, or I'll send a special report to Commander Draukir on your behalf."

Commander Ru'en's jab pulls a chuckle from my throat, and I roll my eyes.

"Right, like you're any less devoted. She saved your hide more times than mine, so—"

"Are you done?"

The fur on my ruff stands on end, both annoyed and wary of the narrowing of Commander Ru'en's eyes.

"Not quite."

He steps closer and raises his hand, obviously prepared to shut me up no matter what it takes. Except, I'm not scared of his fists, even though I know the damage they can do. No, what frightens me is the thought of my little mama—Duri, *not* my little mama—witnessing more violence.

"They still don't understand the dangers we face," I finish in the same breath, eager to diffuse his fury. My stance never falters, never braces for impact, never tenses or cowers, while my attention stays focused on my team leader.

"Then finish the debriefing without waxing poetic."

The urge to fling a knife toward Thret's throat pulls my hand to my hip, but I halt its ascent and cock my head instead.

"I didn't realize you knew such a touching phrase, Thret. Maybe—"

"If you don't want to focus, then I'll finish the lesson," Commander Ru'en snarls.

I spin on my heel and drop into a squat, facing the lamp and ensuring every female in the group can see the seriousness in my gaze.

"The ISC were the white coats who captured you. You know the Intergalactic Science Corps as the largest scientific company in all the known galaxies, but they aren't what they seem. What you saw before you landed on this planet was a ruse. They are evil."

I meet each female's eyes before my attention catches on my little mama's face. Looking away isn't an option—I need to see her expression as I reveal my true lifestyle.

"They experiment on all races in the cruelest of ways. You were their newest acquisitions until we stopped them, and you don't want to know what they might have done to you."

Her lush bottom lip quivers before she firms her expression and squares her shoulders.

"They're an infestation. We're the exterminators. And there's nothing we won't do to end them."

When she glances away, I mourn the loss of both her attention and her trust, the dulling of her eyes conveying how little she respects my line of work.

My heart hardens. I've seen too many atrocities to misunderstand her shudder and shying away—even I hate the things I've witnessed. The failures I've accrued are unforgivable, as are the skills I've honed over the years. My entire life revolves around murder and pain.

A soft, gentle little mama has no place in my world. It's foolish of me to want her.

Yet want her I do.

It hurts to be on the receiving end of her silence. I grit my teeth and suck down a breath before peeling my eyes away from her ashen face.

"So, we'll get you to base camp where you'll be safe, but then we'll continue to hunt them."

Wary stillness permeates from the small group, many of the females clinging to the women around them for support.

"The main issue now is we must do so without alerting both the planet's government and the ISC of our location. They cannot learn the coordinates of our base camp—too many civilians live there, and we won't put them in more danger than they already are."

I wait, letting the battered and tired females process the information. A few moments of quiet pass as even the boy sits without making a sound.

"So, how do we do this?"

My eyes flick to Duri, even though the omega who challenged me at the beginning of the conversation is the one who spoke.

Commander Ru'en answers as I stand and take a few steps back to allow him into the circle of light.

"We keep moving while we wait for a response from command. Do what you need to prepare for travel—we head out in ten minutes."

My gut tightens as I remember how hard the few miles of hiking through the desert was for the omegas, especially my little mama.

Damn it, *not* my little mama.

How can Ru'en expect them to survive a trek through the mountains, especially without food?

Knowing an argument would be futile, I hold in my sigh and cross my arms over my chest, determined to keep a close eye on each one of them and help those who need it most. Even as my instincts demand I pull Duri to me, I refuse to move. I tell myself to stay impartial and subjective, but every time she shifts, my muscles bunch as though to go to her.

I turn to Commander Ru'en and lift a brow, expecting him to issue orders. He doesn't disappoint.

"Refill all three water bags before we leave. There's an exit through the southeast tunnel. Thret will lead, you take their heels, I'll follow and erase any tracks."

A tone beeps through our communicators. We lift our hands in unison and change frequencies.

The somber tone in Jokur's voice tells more than his words.

"We lost target two. Rendezvous or rogue?"

"Rogue. Find supplies. Call when stocked."

Commander Ru'en wastes no time deciding, sending Jokur and Choku off on their own to find supplies for our party before requesting to meet up with us.

Even though we don't know their exact location and they don't know ours, we'll have no trouble finding each other when the time comes to reunite. After years of completing mission after mission, our communication skills surpass most teams, even the other Warrior Elites.

Which is why we were sent to eradicate the tiny ISC hideout in the mountains.

The reminder of such a horrible experience sours my stomach. As the females talk among themselves and suck down water, I tilt my head, requesting a more private location to speak to my teammates.

They oblige, moving into the tunnel toward our original entry point.

"Back in the facility... their experiment focused on the lifemating bond, but what the hell happened? Was it a biological weapon? Should we be worried about infecting these omegas?"

I could rip my own heart from my chest for being so careless. How could I hold such a precious, fragile creature in my arms when there was even the slightest chance of contamination?

The simple answer—I wasn't thinking. I buried the horrifying memories and let my desires rule my actions.

I can't let myself do so again, no matter how much I want to.

Her life, and the child growing in her womb, is too precious to risk.

Chapter Nine

Duri

Why is gravity so cruel? I try to rise onto my knees again but end up lowering myself back onto my butt.

"Here, let me help."

I offer Henna a tight smile and shake my head, which only makes it spin faster.

"No, give me another minute. I'm just not ready yet."

Her strained smile must match my own, because several other omegas turn toward us with concerned expressions. Most are already on their feet, rolling their shoulders and preparing their bodies for the trek with gentle stretches.

Feeling the unease of the others grow as the seconds stretch by and I don't rise, I relax my shoulders and close my eyes, searching deep within my body for hidden stores of energy.

There aren't any. I know this within the very recesses of my soul, but I find my motivation in the soft jabs my baby gives my ribs.

She's healthy. Strong. Growing with every breath I take.

I can't let my weakness be the reason she doesn't get to experience life. Using the nausea as a distraction from the gnawing hunger in my very bones, I give the bottle of pills a squeeze but refuse to look at them.

There are only four left. If I take another now, then what happens if we can't find food? What if it takes more than today and tomorrow to make it to Cahress' base camp?

What if, when we get there, they don't have the technology or resources to make more pills for me?

The thought nearly saps what little control I have away, leaving me eyeing the ground by my hip, wondering if lying down would be better than slumping and hitting my head on the hard stone.

A surprisingly harsh thump on my bladder knocks me out of my semi-panic attack.

I can't focus on the what ifs. All I can do is plan for the next few minutes and live in the now. Firming my spine and caressing my belly, I decide to take another capsule now, but will leave one pill in the container no matter what, so that when we reach safety, they'll have something to duplicate. It's the best I can do since Seung—

I stop my thoughts and open the pill bottle, cramming one capsule in my mouth and taking a swig of water before shoving the container into my pocket and hooking the water hose onto its holder. Even though the nutrition packed into them is more geared toward prenatal requirements than energy supplements, the action fills me with purpose.

I will keep my daughter alive, no matter what it takes.

Henna's tight smile broadens further as I take her offered hand and let her help me to my feet. My nausea grows, but I breathe through my nose and swallow the excess saliva before turning to face the three alphas standing near the back of the cave.

Pale blue eyes steal my attention, the abject misery and extreme self-hatred shining from them sending my heart into my throat. The clenching of my abdominals makes my nausea worse, but I refuse to waste the contents of my stomach.

My feet move forward of their own accord, a thread buried deep within my chest pulling me toward the massive male standing a few feet away.

I need to help him. No one should look so torn and sad, especially not the male who seemed so self-assured and strong mere moments ago.

All expression leaks from his eyes, leaving a cold and remote ghost of himself behind.

"What happened? What's wrong?"

He doesn't move other than to shift his focus to the male beside him.

His disinterest hurts more than I can describe. A chill settles in my bones as I sense the depth of his denial—the link in my chest turns brittle with his icy refusal.

All commonsense melts from my brain as fiery emotions scorch my insides. The instincts which protect my baby double and extend their bubble to include the gigantic brute who refuses to meet my gaze.

I've known him for less than a day, but he won my omega loyalty during the intense interactions.

He was lovely before he sequestered himself away and spoke with his teammates.

Hatred animates me as I turn my attention to Commander Ru'en.

"What did you do?"

White pupils expand and contract as one snowy eyebrow lifts.

"Excuse me?"

Rage colors my vision a shimmery red.

"He was fine before you talked to him. What did you say?"

A hand tugs my elbow backward, but Henna's attempt to pull me away doesn't stand a chance against the fury pulsing through my veins.

Broad shoulders seem to grow broader as Commander Ru'en narrows his gaze on my face. His pupils shrink and hands tighten into fists.

My foot lifts off the ground to close the space between us, the challenge in his stance too much for my incensed omega instincts.

Clear blue orbs arrest my forward moment, the alarm and confusion emanating from Cahress' eyes cutting through my rage.

"What are you doing, Duri?"

Every ounce of anger drains from me, leaving my mind reeling and heart pounding. Pure adrenaline keeps me on my feet.

"I… I don't know. I've never—"

Thret's terrible growl emanates from the pitch-black tunnel behind them, freezing me in place like spotted prey.

"Who is Cahress to you, omega?"

Every muscle in my body locks tight. Not a single thought sneaks into my brain, a great big blank protecting my conscious from whatever he implies.

Commander Ru'en sidesteps and sends me a glare so fierce my arms instinctually wrap around my midsection to protect the precious life within.

Cahress moves his bulk, blocking my view of icy irises and menace. My heart pounds against my sternum as my need to protect the male in front of me insists he turn around. He shouldn't have his back toward danger, and the alpha behind him drips calculated lethality.

"Cahress, is she your lifemate?"

My breath seizes in my lungs as emotions filter through eyes bluer than the sky. Dread settles in my guts as defeat wins over all the others, splintering the brittle cord leading from my chest.

"She can't be. Look at her."

Pain slices deeper than I thought possible, so deep he may as well have torn the very essence of my being into shreds. Instincts awakened by pregnancy scream in agony while my soul bleeds and weeps.

Bile rises into my throat and sandpaper scratches the back of my eyes.

I need to get away. Now.

Lifting my foot to spin on my heel and flee, my clumsiness gets the better of me. My foot hits the edge of a stone and stops mid twist, destroying my balance. I stick my arms out to brace my fall but can't force my hips to straighten to protect my swollen abdomen.

Terror grips my heart and a squeak rips from my throat.

Warm, solid arms wrap around me and stop my descent. I gulp down oxygen and try to hide my shaking, but it grows and grows until my very bones shake.

"I'm sorry! I just—I'm sorry!"

Sobs well up so fast I have no chance of stopping them. Wanting nothing more than to be in the comfort of Cahress' arms, I cling to the bicep pressed against my breasts. His shoulder blocks the right half of my vision as he grips my hip. He stands near my side, with his right arm plastered to my front and his left palm encompassing half my skull while his forearm shields my neck and upper back from whiplash.

It's pathetic, but I tighten my hold on him when he tries to move away.

"I'm—"

"I swear, if you apologize one more time, I'll lose it."

Tears drip onto his arm. My brain replays how stupid and irrational I've been for the last few minutes, but sobs still wrack my body. Now is not the time for such antics. Every second counts, for myself and everyone here, and yet I can't stop crying.

The chest pressed against my temple expands as Cahress takes a deep breath. He exhales and shifts his grip to pull me closer. The wriggling mass of dread loosens its hold on my heart, his actions soothing me more than words.

"I hurt you with my words. I'm sorry. I didn't mean—what I meant was—damn it!"

His arms shift again, pulling me even closer so my side presses flush against his front.

"Aren't you marked, Duri? Surely the alpha who mated you claimed you as well. No worthwhile male would leave an omega so vulnerable."

Embarrassment and anger heat my cheeks. Words clog my throat, but no sounds other than sobs escape my chest.

How can I make them understand when I don't fully understand it myself? I wipe my face with an unsteady hand and shake my head, dislodging his palm from my skull.

It takes three tries before my body responds to my command.

"No, I'm not marked, but it isn't the sire's fault. He was—is—my best friend. Don't talk ill of him. Seung is an amazing alpha, one whom any omega would be proud to call their own, if only—"

My courage falters. I can't reveal Seung's secret, not even if he's dead. Especially if he's dead.

Before I spiral into mourning, I straighten my spine and force my gaze up to meet Cahress' clear blue eyes.

"I couldn't tie him to me when his heart belonged elsewhere."

For two wonderful seconds, Cahress' gentle purr vibrates through me, but he stops himself and slides his arm free of my clenched fingers. His massive palms settle on my shoulders and hold me an arm's length away from him.

The distance between us hurts.

He opens his mouth, but Commander Ru'en speaks before he forms words.

"This changes nothing. You can't claim her, Cahress. You shouldn't even be touching her."

Agitation grows behind my sternum as the strong arms wrapped around me loosen. I try to fix my grip, only to find myself standing alone.

"He's right. There's too much at risk. This is bigger than you and I."

"What?"

"I'm sorry, Duri. I'll do my best to stay away from you. Let the other alphas help you when you need it."

Without a backward glance, he turns and stalks down the corridor, hitting Thret's shoulder with his own as he disappears into the darkness. The leashed fury in the contact reverberates through the surrounding stone, and despite the scant light from the lantern, my eyes refuse to stop searching for his massive frame.

Time passes, how much I can't say, but Henna tugs my elbow and guides me into the hall. With Hayden and his mother in front of us and the rest of the omegas behind us, we stumble through the tunnel until the last rays of the sunset grace the path ahead.

Steep, uneven steps lead out of the cave and down around the corner. I use Henna's forearm and the jagged wall to keep my balance, embracing the odd numbness Cahress left behind when he walked away.

It's irrational—I've only known him for a handful of hours—but his rejection hurts just as much as the visual of Seung's limp body hanging between two white-clad forms.

My heel slips on an unexpectedly smooth stone, but I slap the wall and regain my balance, hissing as I cut my hand on the rocks.

The reminder of my surroundings pulls me from my useless ruminations. A fall down these stairs could prove deadly, especially if the expanse of open air means a cliff on the other side of the bend. I shake my hand to ward off the sting and nod at Henna, letting her know I'm alright before straightening my spine and lowering my foot to the next step.

Something pops in my pelvic floor, startling a gasp from me. I let go of Henna and lean my forearm against the wall, hunching forward in hopes to prevent further strain on whatever I must have injured.

Except no pain emerges.

No, something worse happens.

Thick liquid floods my panties. Screaming internally at the unfairness of it all, skyrocketing into panic, I gather my skirt between my legs and press the ball of fabric against my womanhood.

The synthetic plug broke.

I can't do this. Seung's scent fills my nostrils and breaks my hold on reality.

The chances of my baby's survival, as well as my own, just drastically decreased.

My heart hurts too much for this.

I sink to my bottom and cover my face with one hand while pushing my skirt so hard against the apex of my thighs that pain streaks into my clit.

Tears coat my face as seed soaks my skirt.

Chapter Ten

Cahress

Physical pain radiates up my thighs as I fight the urge to dart up the stairs, the little mama's feet skidding on pebbles making me want to go to her. As pebbles skitter down the steps, I glance over my shoulder and see Duri righting herself with the help of her partner. I turn and step closer to the ledge, about to lean around the corner and check the area, but a squeak freezes me in place. I battle against the urge to sprint back the way I came and scoop my little mama into my arms.

No, not mine.

Yet. Not mine *yet*.

Her admission changes *everything*. It explains why I can't stop thinking about her. Why I want her. Why my soul yearns to merge with hers.

She's my lifemate, unmarked and ripe for my claiming. Fate built us for each other: we're meant to be together.

But the revelation makes our situation more dire. I can't claim her until we're somewhere safe.

Her gut-wrenching sob lifts my boot from the stone floor and propels me back into the cave. Small figures block my path as the omegas gather around my little mama. Thret's glare stomps closer as he prepares to haul me away, but I step to the side and put the group between us. It won't stop him should he decide I need intervention, but it'll give me an extra half a second to react.

Voices talk over one another, their worried tones turning frantic.

"Duri! What's—"

"Is that—"

"Oh no."

"Her waters broke!"

I grab slim shoulders and lift the nearest omega out of my way, setting her down as gently as I can with urgency pulsing through my body.

The moment my hands rest on the next impeding female, the overall emotion within the cave flips. Every female backs away as quickly as she can, the one in front of me bumping against my hip in her haste to retreat.

Alarm yanks me into action. I push the omega to the side and lunge forward only to stand toe to toe with an angry alpha.

A tense moment passes, time standing still as I prepare to battle Thret. No one moves as silence settles over us.

Duri's muffled sob lifts the fur on my nape, but before I slam my knife into Thret's stomach, Henna speaks.

"Her waters didn't break, but she smells like alpha. The scent is too strong—I'm sorry, I can't—"

Her choked gag accompanies the sound of shuffling feet as the omegas instinctually move further away. The terrible knot in my chest loosens as I realize she isn't in immediate mortal danger, but the news brings confusion as well.

I look over Thret's shoulder but can't see her tiny frame since she's sitting. My teammate mirrors my movement, blocking my view again.

"She needs help, damnit."

My snarl bounces off the rock walls, making the females flinch and the boy cower behind his mother, but Thret doesn't so much as blink.

"She does, but not from you."

The harsh reminder of our predicament both infuriates and calms me. I take a deep breath, resentful of the scentless air brought to me by my suit, and slide my knife back into its holster.

Just because I must keep my physical distance from her doesn't mean I can't help her.

"Little mama, are you hurt?"

She sniffles, bites back a sob, then sniffs again before speaking in a shaky voice full of turmoil.

"No, I'm not hurt."

"What happened?"

"The plug popped free."

Thret's furrowed brow matches my own, and a glance over his shoulder reveals Commander Ru'en's puzzled expression as well. I gather my wits and continue, desperate to understand.

"What plug?"

"An artificial knot. It kept Seung's s—oh gods, I can't—"

Understanding dawns like a lightbulb being flicked on. Omegas need regular mating throughout their pregnancy, or the fetus won't survive. Instinct and the mating mark usually keep couples close together in such times, but it's been over twenty-four hours since the crash. And she's not mated.

But an artificial knot? I never thought something like that would exist—and by the look on my teammates' faces, neither did they.

"It's okay, Duri. Take deep breaths and calm down. Can you do that, little mama?"

If she nods, I can't see her, but the slight dilation of Ru'en's white pupils tell me she's trying.

"I think I understand, but only you know exactly what this means. Only you can tell us what needs to be done. So, take a few more calming breaths and talk to me, yes?"

"Okay."

Her soft whisper nearly cracks my heart in two. I pour strength and comfort into the thread between our hearts, needing to help her in any way I can.

"Usually a plug lasts three or four days, but I guess the trauma of the last few hours weakened it. But—"

There isn't much power behind her voice, but she sounds much steadier than she did a few moments ago. She takes an audible breath and forges onward.

"I also take supplements, usually only twice a day, to make sure my baby gets the nutrients it needs. I was in the infirmary when the ship went down, but I didn't have time to refill my prescription, so with the stress and dehydration and—and everything, I... I only have four left."

Commander Ru'en crosses his arms over his chest and studies the female I wish with every fiber of my being to lay eyes on. My words emerge from a thick throat, the defeat in her tone scaring me more than I care to admit.

"How many have you taken since the crash?"

"Two, both after we entered the cave. And I'm still so dizzy and tired."

I can't stand the pain and desperation dripping from her every word. Shifting my gaze to meet white pupils and black irises, I let my emotions shine from my eyes before narrowing my focus on the brute in front of me.

"Move, or I'll kill you."

"You'll try."

"I'll win."

Commander Ru'en addresses the group of omegas behind me, ignoring my threats.

"Who else came into contact with any of our suits?"

A few timid voices echo through the cave.

"Check your skin. Evaluate your body. Does anyone have symptoms beyond what you'd expect from yesterday's excursion?"

Gods, why the hell am I so dense? The need to hold my little mama overrides my common sense—and my focus. Before she blew my mind with her revelation, I refused to touch her for fear of infecting her with residual chemicals or such from our previous mission.

Commander Ru'en does his best to alleviate my fear.

He points at Henna, making the omega shrink despite how far away he stands from her.

"You had prolonged exposure to Cahress' suit. List your current symptoms."

She straightens her shoulders but doesn't release her white knuckled grip on the female beside her.

"Headache, sore muscles, bruises, and sore feet. And I'm hungrier than I've been in my entire life."

Commander Ru'en nods at her before pinning me in place with an almost impassive stare, which proves far softer than his normal menace.

"It's idiotic to fight the urge to be near your lifemate, so you're going to tend her, but you will not mark her until we get to base camp. Maybe not even then, if command deems it so. Understand?"

Excitement and eagerness vibrate through every cell in my body, setting my bones to buzzing. I tilt my chin, acknowledging his logic, and flex my fingers in anticipation of touching my omega.

"If I so much as suspect you intend to take off your face mask, I'll tranq you and leave you where you lie. Understand?"

"Yes, I understand."

He uncrosses his arms and rests the palm of his left hand on the tranquilizer, his message clear. I nod and raise an eyebrow as I shift my gaze to Thret, still primed for a fight should the dense alpha refuse to move.

"If she tries to mark you, I'm bashing your head in and hogtying her until we get to base camp."

Thret's gravelly words pull a growl from me, his open disgust and fury as he threatens my little mama too much for my already threadbare control. The world slows as I jab my knife at his abdomen.

He knocks my wrist with his forearm and steps to the side in the same motion, using my own momentum to propel me past him. Half a step later, I snap my blade back into its holster and drop down beside Duri. All thoughts of violence disappear, my need to comfort and care for this tiny omega washing away every other urge.

Not sure what she needs, I slide a hand onto her slender shoulder and lean forward, shielding her from the world as best as I can in my squatting position. Rich brown eyes meet mine, my own yearning and fear reflected back at me from her gaze.

"What do you need, little mama?"

"Do we have any feminine products? I need to keep his seed inside me as long as possible."

Despite her sunburnt face and blotchy skin from crying, her blush shows clearly on her naturally pale cheeks. I glance at both of my teammates and start to shake my head in response, but an idea stops me.

"I have sterile cloth bandages. Will that work?"

Her blush deepens, but she nods in affirmation. I slip several small, flat squares from random pockets in my chest harness and pants, gathering a stack of five before offering them to her.

She doesn't move to take them. Her eyes bounce around the cave before landing on me with a pleading expression.

"I... um..."

"Need help?"

Her eyes widen and panic emanates from her. She lifts the hand not hidden between her legs and pushes at my arm, shaking her head vehemently.

"No! No, I need privacy."

Gods, I'm such an idiot. Still, her mortification confuses me. She's a pregnant omega, not an untried innocent.

"Will you be ready to travel afterward?"

Commander Ru'en breaks the bubble of intimacy my mind erected around Duri and myself. I bite back my snarl when light brown irises turn away from my gaze and meet my team leader's face. Her far-off expression helps me curb my desire to lunge across the tunnel and rip the other alpha to pieces for stealing my omega's attention. She isn't focused on him—she's deep in thought.

"Every doctor I've seen since the start of my pregnancy told me the same thing—since I'm not bonded and didn't have proper care during the first few weeks, I won't survive if I don't take the supplements twice a day or have fresh alpha seed. My baby takes more nutrients from me than a normal pregnancy, so without either of those two substances, my body will fail and both myself and the baby will die."

My heart seizes in my chest at the thought, but she shakes herself free of her thoughts and stares directly into my soul.

"Will you carry me after I finish? Walking will only make me lose—"

"Yes. Without hesitation."

Tears fill her gorgeous eyes, morphing them to shimmery swirls of deep brown.

"Thank you."

"My pleasure, little mama."

I mean it to the depths of my soul.

The sounds of footsteps fade as the rest of our party head out into the night, Commander Ru'en instructing me to catch up as quickly as possible before he disappears around the corner.

When nothing but our breathing fills the air, Duri slips the packages from my fingers and gnaws on her bottom lip. I stroke her shoulder before guiding her onto her back, the stairs keeping her head higher than her feet.

She looks between her hands and my face several times before her blush steals down her neck and distracts me by coloring the upper slope of her breasts. Even through her blouse and undergarment, her nipples create little peaks.

"Will you... turn your back?"

With her hair creating a halo around her head and her legs bare from her bunched skirt, the urge to worship her with teeth and tongue nearly strip me of my control. My covered palm lifts and caresses the enticing underside of her belly.

Her whimper freezes me in place.

Chapter Eleven

Duri

Just the gentle glide of his thick digits over my protruding belly sends electricity through my abdomen. Little flutters play against his broad fingers, stealing my breath as wonder shines from masculine eyes.

I want to bask in the moment, but stone stabs my back and my arm aches from holding my skirt between my legs.

"Please?"

Regret tightens the skin around his eyes, but he nods and removes his hand before standing. He pauses before yanking something from his pocket and setting it beside my hip. I read the label on the bottle and nod, thankful to have something to clean my hands.

He turns his back to me, so I drop the packets onto my breasts, clench my thighs together to hold my skirt in place, sanitize my hands, and open the packets. Rolling the gauze into a makeshift tampon, I struggle to find a position where I won't lose precious time during insertion but can't move much with the bundle of fabric mashed against my crotch.

I squeak when gloved hands wrap around my ankles. Light blue eyes send my heart galloping as he lifts a brow in a devilish, tempting smile so wonderful it steals my breath despite his mask hiding his lips from my gaze.

"Trust me?"

His simple request arrows into my soul. I nod, my decision made without thought.

He lifts my ankles and sits with his back toward me, propping both of my legs on one shoulder.

"Tell me when you're ready and I'll move your right ankle to my other shoulder. I won't peek, promise."

The black fabric covering his head hides his hair. I want to snarl and rip the offending material away but suck down a breath and focus on the bundle of joy in my abdomen.

"I'm ready."

True to his word, he keeps his eyes trained away and his back facing me as he ducks his head and pulls my right ankle to his other shoulder. I grit my teeth and yank my skirt up with my left hand and press the rolled cloth deep into my body with the right.

My clit pulses in need, but I ignore it, cramming my fingers even deeper until my knuckles sink past my entrance.

The dry cotton expands as it absorbs slick and seed. I jiggle it around, making sure it lodges in place before slipping my hand free and covering my legs with my wet skirt.

Bittersweet emotions threaten to drown me in tears as Seung's scent invades my nostrils. A drop slips from my lashes, but I twist and sanitize my hands using the bottle beside me.

Gentle digits lower my legs to the ground before masculine arms surround me. I cling to his harness, wishing I could rub my cheek on his bare chest and fill my nose with his scent. Even though I have no idea what he smells like, I know without a doubt I'll enjoy his potent pheromones.

"Ready?"

"Yes."

His smooth gait lulls me into a much calmer state. I watch as the stars twinkle in the cloudless sky, not bothering to keep track of our surroundings as Cahress stalks through the mountains.

"Cahress?"

His gentle hum disrupts the purr I didn't even realize I floated in, but I push past the haze of bliss and reach for cognitive thoughts.

"Why are the other alphas so against us bonding?"

"They aren't. Not personally, anyway—except for maybe Thret. He's always been…"

Luminescent blue eyes reflect the starlight as it shimmers off the rocks, Cahress shaking his head ruefully before he changes the course of his thoughts.

"We have reason to believe the ISC is experimenting on the lifemating bond. The Alpha Elites—a group of human alphas—killed the previous ISC leader because he targeted their lifemates."

His low voice carries no further than my ears, but he gentles his tone further as though to hide the terrible message in his next words.

"Warrior Elite Team 1 all found their lifemates while on mission in Mai'CuS, and all were attacked. We don't know how or why, but we can't risk being so vulnerable when we're away from base camp."

He jumps over a crack in the path and lifts his arms while he bends his neck, nuzzling the top of my head with his chin.

"I can't promise to wait until we have our own den. My chest hurts from wanting you."

My bones melt and heat sweeps through my core. I press my cheek against his shoulder and shiver, torn between a sense of self-dislike and joy.

He's too big and brash and strong, yet he's perfect. I want him.

Which makes me a terrible friend and mother. I should focus on getting my babe to safety. I should scream and wail and beg this behemoth to find my best friend.

A gush of warmth flows from between my legs. Terror grips my heart, tensing my entire body.

"What's wrong?"

"It didn't work."

"What?"

"The bandages didn't work."

Nothing but the wind howling over stone marks the passing of time as Cahress closes the distance between us and the group. He sends a dark look toward Commander Ru'en, glancing at me and shaking his head. Silent communication passes between the two of them before Commander Ru'en nods and scales up the slope to our right. The deadly alpha traverses the veritable cliff face with ease, moving over the omegas and dropping beside Thret on silent feet.

"You're okay, Duri. We'll do whatever it takes to get you to safety. Just relax against me and tell me if you start feeling worse. Sip some water."

I follow his command, overstimulation sending me into a pit of numbness. My exhaustion, both emotional and physical, win over my desire to stay alert. I slip into a doze as he follows the stumbling group of omegas.

When my eyelids flutter open, I notice the lightening of the sky and fight against the scream building behind my sternum. Since Cahress cradles me to his chest, I don't know how much has dripped from my womanhood, but the fabric pressed against my folds chills my intimates.

Which means it's been a while since the last bit of seed left my insides.

I've no doubt left a trail. What if we're being followed?

No, surely the alphas would have thought of that.

"How do you feel?"

Cahress' voice whisks away my panic, but my tongue sticks to the roof of my mouth. I pull the straw to my lips and take a tiny sip before responding.

"Tired. How long was I asleep?"

"A few hours."

"How many?"

"Almost six."

A wave of dizziness makes my fingers clench around the mouthpiece and nausea tightens my stomach.

"Take another pill, then get some more rest."

My fingers shake as I reach into my pocket, my skirt crunchy in some places and sticky in others. I ignore the discomfort and struggle to open the container. My digits don't want to cooperate, and a well of emptiness opens under me, sucking my energy into a dark abyss.

A deep rumble vibrates into my bones, my alpha purring as he walks. I pinch a pill between two fingers and slide it onto my tongue, pressing my lips together as I close the container. Wedging the container back into my pocket, I suck down some water and swallow the pill.

The usual sense of relief doesn't come.

I find no reprieve from the energy-sucking abyss.

"Make me take another in four hours. Please, Cahress."

"No. Take another now. I didn't realize you felt so bad, or I would have woken you earlier."

"Is there food? Are we safe?"

An edge of warning sneaks into his purr, but my body remains limp as my mind processes his anger.

"No and no but take another. My other teammates found a secure hiding place and some supplies, so we'll meet with them in an hour or two."

His voice sounds far away, even though I feel his chest moving against my arm. When I speak, my own words sound muffled, as though there's cotton stuffed into my ears.

"Other teammates?"

"Yes, Jokur and Choku. We separated at the crash site."

"Seung?"

A long pause carries nothing but wind and the ever constant, smooth rocking of my alpha's footsteps.

"They don't have any survivors with them."

A tear slips from my eye, but for the life of me I can't remember closing my lids, nor can I force them to lift.

"Duri?"

Tiny thumps along my ribs and the fluttering of life within my womb steady me against the flood of mourning threatening to push me into the abyss. As tempting as the peace of the darkness is, I yank myself back from the ledge and hum in response to Cahress.

"Take another pill. Please."

I intend to nod my acquiescence but end up nuzzling against his firm pectoral instead. He murmurs something over my head, his tone clipped with alarm. The world stops moving and warmth surrounds me, erasing the chill of the wind.

Familiar noises sound—fabric rustling, pills clacking against plastic, the water hose sliding against Cahress' suit—but they don't mean anything until something presses against my lips. I part my teeth and accept the pill before closing my mouth around the end of the water hose. After forcing myself to swallow two mouthfuls of water, I turn my head away from the hose and sigh as my stomach accepts the offering.

The abyss shrinks, still lingering under me but not so close to the soles of my feet, and when I open my eyes, I greet sky blue orbs with a small smile.

"Better?"

"A little, yes, thank you."

"Still so polite. Hang in there, little mama. We'll stop soon."

"Okay."

I couldn't move if I wanted to. Every ounce of my energy goes toward keeping my child alive, the happy flips and kicking of her fragile body within mine enough to block out the worry of the world while I focus on breathing.

Woven within my tiny bubble of existence, a masculine purr erases the angst constantly tapping at my subconscious. With the trauma of the last few hours and the uncertainty of the future, I find only three things matter most to me.

The first is my child. She means more than even I do. She *is* the future.

My heart reveals the second most important thing as the alpha carrying me now. Without him, I will never feel whole. He's the other half of my heart, the peace within the storm, the protector I've always yearned for. He's my lifemate, pure and simple.

And the third? Seung. A lifetime of friendship cannot be forgotten. Whatever I can do, however I can help him, I must do it.

The slow rising of the sun heats the exposed half of my face, but I don't bother to shield myself. I cycle between dozing and watching the covered chin of the male ferrying me over the mountains, fragmented thoughts slowly coming together. With his attention elsewhere, I allow myself to feel the depths of my emotions for him.

I know what must come next, but I'm not ready for it.

Chapter Twelve

Cahress

Commander Ru'en nods and falls back to the rear of the party. I lengthen my stride and quicken my pace, closing the distance between Duri and the temporary safe room Jokur and Choku created.

The limp form in my arms urges me to move faster. I count every second as it passes, sensing just how close she is to slipping into a coma. If she falls asleep and can't wake up, I have no way to help her.

I glance down and meet glazed brown eyes, relieved to see her still awake. Boulders whiz by in a blur as I sprint through a maze of stone and sand, until Choku steps onto the path and gestures toward a narrow offshoot. As unassuming as the other thousands of pathways, I notice the red striations within the rock for the first time as I squeeze between the boulders, the layering of different colors intriguing.

Weaving my way through the path as it twists and turns, I ignore the sense of claustrophobia as the walls on either side grow taller and random outcroppings of stone block out the sun. Between one stride and the next, I find myself in an unlikely open space as the tight passageway spills into a canyon. One side boasts intricate carvings and darkened doors, the shapes crafted several feet into the rock, making it invisible from above. The other walls look no different from every other ledge and boulder within the biome, leading me to believe whatever community built this structure wanted to remain hidden.

Which is exactly what we need.

I hurry to the second largest door and follow the coded instructions Jokur sent a few minutes ago, not waiting for my eyes to adjust after I step into the dark. After several minutes of walking, the tunnel splits in two. I follow the path to the left and duck into the first small opening on the left.

Propped against the wall next to a small pile of goods, Jokur wastes no time in tossing a meal packet to me. It wounds my soul to lift my hand away from Duri, but I catch the item and nod before sitting in the far corner of the cave.

As gently as I can, I lower my little mama into my lap and rearrange her into what I hope is a comfortable position. The moment I lift my hands from her, I rip open a corner of the packet and squeeze the food toward the hole, hoping it doesn't taste too terrible cold.

My gloved finger teases her bottom lip, the digit going rogue before I recall it to my side. Half a second later, it brushes her hair from her face and strokes her scalp in long, soothing caresses.

"Open your mouth, little mama. Time to eat."

Her eyelashes flutter and her chest expands on an uneven breath before she nods and accepts the first bite of food. I wait until she swallows to offer her more, but there's no stopping my hand as it pets and praises her.

As the food slowly disappears, her breathing becomes less labored and color returns to her cheeks. When I stop running my fingers through her hair to squeeze the last few bites of food closer to the hole, a feminine rumble makes my heart skip a beat and my lips lift in a smirk.

She doesn't like when I stop petting her.

"Hush, Duri. Just a little more food, then I can give you all my attention."

"You aren't already?"

The whimsical lilt in her tone reveals just how removed from reality she is at the moment. I chuckle and offer her more food.

"Not even close. I have so much more I want to give you."

A beautiful thickness enters her growl, morphing the sound to one of pleasure instead of annoyance. My shaft hardens within my suit, sending streaks of pain through my shaft. I lock my muscles in place, abhorring the idea of ending such a sweet and tantalizing moment because I can't handle my wayward cock.

"No one has ever made me feel the way you do. Don't stop, Cahress, please. Even if I pull away, don't stop."

My hand pauses with my fingertips poised over her hairline, ready to delve into her long raven locks. Her plea sends shivers down my spine, lifting my ruff, but the worry tinting her tone confuses me.

"Why would you pull away?"

"I'm scared."

"Scared of what?"

"Everything."

She has every right to be scared. Her spaceship crashed. The ISC kidnapped her. She's in a cave in the middle of nowhere with strange alphas, pregnant and vulnerable.

But she's speaking of something specific to our discussion—us. Our time together.

"Are you scared of me?"

"No, but..." her breath stutters as she lifts her lids and studies me in the faint lantern light, "You're so big and I'm so small."

I run my fingers over her scalp, setting up the rhythm she enjoys.

"Yes, we are quite different, aren't we?"

Her focus narrows to my eyes as though she searches for a specific answer.

"H-have you ever..."

She closes her mouth and shakes her head, not intending to continue.

"Have I ever?" I prod, needing to understand what's going on in her gorgeous mind.

"Have you ever knotted an omega?"

The question pulls a blush into her cheeks, lending a sweet innocence to her face. Worried she'll think the worst of me, but unable to lie to her, I tell her the truth.

"Several times, yes. In my culture, it's customary for an alpha to service an omega every other rut for the first five years after they present their dynamic. I was ten years past maturity when the ISC attacked my family."

Slim shoulders tense and her dainty brow furrows, but the worry pursing her lips recedes, leaving her mouth lush and tempting.

"But..."

"But?" I repeat, urging her to ask whatever is on her mind.

"But you never marked anyone?"

"No, little mama. I'm not bonded."

"So, the females on your planet... is it normal for them to be pregnant and unclaimed?"

The question slaps me upside the head.

"I'd never thought about it, but yes."

A corner of her mouth ticks up before she murmurs, more to herself than to me.

"No wonder you haven't balked at my current state. I wish I'd been born on your planet."

Unhappiness tightens her lips, and she shakes her head again, dislodging whatever thought strikes her. She changes tactics, squaring her shoulders and trailing her palms in little circles on her swollen abdomen. Both movements make my turgid cock pulse within its confines.

"Where I'm from, the government strictly regulates all things pertaining to reproduction. Omegas spend their heats in a medically induced coma unless they request otherwise. If Seung hadn't agreed to service me, I would have had to sleep through my first heat."

To give myself time to process her words, I offer her the water and watch her delicate throat work as she swallows. My damn cock jerks in want at the visual delight.

"You've only had one heat?"

She almost chokes on the water, but I pull the mouthpiece away and skim my finger over her reddened cheek. Her nod confirms her answer.

"Was it wild and raw?"

My question causes her to choke on air, lust making my voice deeper and rougher than I intend. The thought of her in the throes of estrous, writhing and needy, supersede the visual of another alpha leaning over her, and even though I didn't intend to ask such a visceral question, I can't help but need an answer.

"What?"

Her wide, startled eyes aren't the response I expected.

"Did you build a nest just so you could destroy it in the throes of rutting? Did you pull him close and beg him to knot you? Slick all over his face and thighs?"

Petite fingers dart up and press against the lower half of my mask, shushing me as her face scarlet. She trembles in my lap.

"Stop! N-no, nothing like that!"

Her arm drops back to her lap, revealing how weak she feels.

"Then how was it?"

"The nurse buckled me to the rutting table and a few hours later, Seung came in and serviced me."

"How exactly did he service you?"

Even in the dim light, her cheeks grow redder as her blush deepens.

"He rutted and knotted me."

"Did he touch you with his hands?"

"Yes."

"Other than to grab your hips?"

Her eyes fill with tears and conflicting emotions warp her features.

"No, but why would he?"

A curse slips from my lips. How could such a stunning omega be pregnant and yet so innocent?

"Because alphas love to pleasure omegas. To see a female fly apart under your mouth and hands is the most fulfilling thing to an alpha's ego."

"Maybe for you, but Seung isn't like that."

"Every alpha is like that, whether he wants to admit it or not."

"Not Seung."

The quiver of her chin works in time with the shimmer of her eyes as she stares at me with such heartbreak I long to believe her.

"How do you know?"

"Because Seung likes men."

The admission breaks a dam within her. Words spill from between her clenched teeth as tears trail down her temples.

"We've known each other almost our entire lives, have been close friends since we learned to walk, and so when he told me he desired a male omega, I wanted him to find the perfect match. Except there are no male omegas on Ko'ea. There are no same gender pairs on my planet."

Her breath hitches, but she plows on as though her heart will break if she doesn't finish her story.

"And so I saved every cent I could for almost four years so he could relocate to a new world. Knowing he would leave me and find his happily ever after, I asked him for one thing before he left. But he would've done it anyway, just because he loves me."

I gather her close, wanting to absorb every ounce of pain emanating from her.

"I was so selfish, and now he's in danger because of me! He shouldn't have come on the cruise—"

"Hush, Duri. No one could have predicted your ship would crash."

As I say the words, a knot forms in my stomach. What if the crash wasn't an accident? If the ISC was behind so many other lifemate pairs meeting on Mai'CuS, then why couldn't they be the puppet masters behind this debacle?

Logical thought deems the idea ludicrous, but instincts declare it to be true.

And Warrior Elite don't ignore the instincts they've honed through years on the battlefield.

I glance up and meet Jokur's intelligent eyes, seeing the same thought echoed in his expanded pupils before he turns to the door. Thret ducks through the low opening, a tiny frame held in his arms. The boy's mother follows on his heels, taking the child's sleeping form before she sits against the wall near the pile of supplies.

As the rest of the party files into the space, I begin a quiet purr and run my glove through Duri's hair, wishing I could feel the strands against my flesh. When she relaxes against me, I check her breathing and pulse before requesting another high calorie meal packet from Jokur. He tosses one over the heads of the omegas huddled in the center of the room before resuming his job of parceling out the rest of the supplies.

Commander Ru'en crouches through the entry and taps the side of his fist against a disc to the left of the doorway. A grid of red lights appears over the opening, effectively locking us away from the rest of the world.

"Where did you find that?" Thret asks Jokur, pointing to the grid.

"We ran a few circles around a convoy a few miles northeast."

"What else did you find?"

I listen and create a running catalogue as my teammates list the items available, but I devote the bulk of my attention to the tiny female in my arms. She accepts a few more bites of food but turns her head away before she consumes even a quarter of the packet.

I want to push her to eat more, but tension pulls her features tight, and when I offer her the water straw, she refuses to open her mouth.

"What's wrong, little mama?"

"Nauseous."

I strengthen my purr despite the uneasy glances the other omegas give me.

"How can I help?"

Her hand shifts closer to her pocket, so I sink my fingers into the fabric and pull out the bottle of pills.

Only two remain.

Chapter Thirteen

Duri

I latch onto his wrist as best as I can, the circumference too wide to wrap my fingers around. Even the small movement leaves me feeling as though I ran a mile through the desert.

I shouldn't have let myself get so worked up. My outburst stole whatever energy the food should have given me.

"One has to stay in the bottle."

Pale blue eyes glance my way before he nods and presses the second to last pill against my lips, his movements so efficient and quick I can't track them.

"Take this one now. You need it."

The angst in my chest vibrates from his throat, the thread tying us together frightening in its impact despite not being fully formed. How intense will our bond be once we mark each other?

I yearn to experience everything he can give me—I've always wanted a true lifemating bond—but life and circumstances always made my dream seem silly and unreachable. Now, even with him so close, I still can't join him the way my soul wants.

It isn't fair.

The pill helps ease my nausea, but as my body absorbs the nutrients Cahress so gently fed me, a new hunger wakens. My clit pulses and slick gathers on my folds as heat builds in my core.

The incessant lust of raging hormones rears its ugly head, reminding me of how ravenous my body has been since the beginning of my pregnancy. During the fight for survival, my organs blocked the desire for stimulation, but now, with the male my soul pleads for so near, the roaring inferno consumes my blood.

Frightening in its intensity, a cramp steals through my abdomen.

Wetness seeps into my skirt.

A whine slips from my throat.

"What's wrong, little mama?"

"It isn't enough."

"Then eat some more—"

His eyes narrow in wariness, the small patch of flesh revealed by his mask crinkling with his surprise as a nasty sound rumbles from my chest.

"I don't want food!"

Frustration drips from my lashes as embarrassment grits my teeth together. How can I act so childish, so selfish, when he's done his best to care for me?

Smooth fabric wipes my tears away as he counters my snarl with a lovely, deep purr of his own. I relax under his hands, the heat of lust lowering to a simmer with the mere brush of his gloved fingers over my face.

Gods, it's not enough, but it's more than anyone else has ever given me.

"Hush, sweet omega. Calm down and tell me what you need."

Incredulity runs through me. I blink my tears away and search what little his mask doesn't hide of his face. Annoyed at the covering, my words come out harsher than I intend.

"You know what I need better than I do."

The skin beside his right eye crinkles, indicating another devilish smirk tilts his lips.

"I think I do, but I need to hear you say the words. I won't cross this line without knowing you understand."

His hands stop caressing my face and scalp, leaving me bereft and at the mercy of the raging fire. I shake with hunger.

"Touch me, Cahress. Touch every part of me."

His purr drops to a sinful pitch, eliciting another cramp deep in my abdomen. Slick floods my skirt and fills his lap, and my hips tilt of their own accord, rubbing my bottom against the alarmingly enormous shaft trapped against his inner thigh.

"Your body needs what only I can give it, doesn't it? It needs my seed. My strength. My domination."

"Yes, please."

My whine surprises me, since I've never heard myself so desperate. Even during my heat, I couldn't form words with the protective strap over my mouth, and now, even though I'm not in estrous and other people sit nearby, I writhe and plead like a woman gone mad.

"Hang on, Duri. I can't give you what you need here. Sip some water while I take you someplace safe."

My fingers close around the hose as he surges to his feet. His lithe grace fills me with the need to worship him. To obey him. To give him everything.

I slip the mouthpiece between my teeth and sip almost absently, distracted by the bunching and flexing of his muscles as he picks his way through the crowded room. Masculine voices converse, but the only attention I give them is a curled lip as Cahress pauses his purr to respond.

Darkness steals my vision until a snapping sound gives way to a yellow glow. Cahress sets the little stick of chemicals on a nearby rock, revealing a space barely big enough for my alpha to fit lying flat on his back. A red glow joins the yellow as he engages a laser grid over the doorway.

How did such a massive male fit through that tiny opening, especially with me in his arms?

He settles me into his lap with his back pressed against the far wall. I release the straw, not caring where it lands despite how important water is to my survival.

Large digits sweep my hair from my face and massage my scalp until what little remains of my logical thoughts leak from my toes and disappears beyond the stone floor. My eyelids slip lower, blocking my view of mesmerizing pale blue orbs, so I force them upward and lift my hand to touch his chest.

I falter an inch away from his suit, the intimidating harness a stark reminder of my beast's deadly skills. He leans away and unclips the harness and underlying vest, sliding them off his shoulders and placing them carefully on the floor beside him. Without the bulky material, the skin-tight black fabric of his suit highlights the dips and bulges of his muscles, sending a thrill up my spine and a cramp through my abdomen.

Before I finish my perusal, he delves his fingers into my hair and scrambles my senses. I arch into his touch, so needy I don't realize he unbuttoned my shirt and released the clip at the front of my bra until the smooth fabric of his glove traces from the upper swell of my exposed right breast to my sternum. The glide of warm cloth as he teases a line down the center of my chest both annoys and enchants me.

His name leaves my lips on a groan.

"I know, little mama, but wait. Listen to me," he traps my chin between his fingers, leaving my chest cold after his scorching touch, and angles my face to meet his.

"I can't take my mask off. The moment I scent you, I'll mark and knot you *for days*. We aren't safe enough for that here."

Impatience and joy war within my veins, his words beautiful and enticing and so very perfect.

My ribs hurt from the strength of my purr. I want him. Now.

"Duri..."

His eyes close as he savors my rumble with a bittersweet expression tightening the flesh between his eyes.

"This will be wild and raw, like I promised. Let go and trust me. I'll take care of you afterward, I promise."

With his words lingering in the air, he turns to the tiny pack I didn't notice sitting by his knee and pulls out several articles of clothing. He spreads the old but surprisingly clean shirts and pants on the ground in a hasty form of bedding before lowering me on top. The layers of fabric do little to buffer me from the cold of the rocks, but at least the sharp edges don't dig into my spine.

None of it matters as he looms over me, my savior in the pits of hell both guarding and terrorizing me in the same instant.

He doesn't touch me. Doesn't ease the raging wildfire gaining ground in my nerve endings. Doesn't offer the comfort of his arms.

Instead, he pinches the tip of his finger and slides his glove off his hand.

Potent alpha pheromones fill my nostrils and hijack my body. Slick gushes from my womanhood as my core contracts and my clit throbs, the amount of wetness even more than during estrous. His heady, salty scent fills my mind's eye with visions of puffy white clouds in a bright blue sky as waves roll through an ocean so expansive it covers the entire horizon. I want to jump into the sea and drown in his depths after soaring through the clouds.

His other glove joins the first, the slap of fabric on stone barely registering above his delectable purr.

My eyes roll to the back of my head as thick, callused fingers cup my breasts and pluck my nipples, both stoking and calming the heat coursing through my veins. He strokes and pinches and tortures my sensitive flesh with strong, skilled digits, wringing needy sounds from between my clenched teeth.

One hand glides up over my collarbone and teases the vulnerable column of my throat before he spans his fingers around the base of my skull and caresses my chin with his thumb. His other hand lowers to my round midsection and ghosts a gentle sweep of his palm around the delicate new life growing within, adoration apparent with every shift of his fingers.

I need to hold on to something before I spiral into madness. My arms lift and I grab whatever I can reach, but his suit makes gripping his massive muscles impossible. As his digits slip under the waistband of my skirt, he ducks down and releases my face to yank the top half of his mask off his head.

His scent blasts across my senses, sending another wave of slick onto my thighs, and my hands shoot to the softest hair imaginable. Almost too dense to weave my fingers into, I knead and hum and explore the newly revealed fur atop his head, skimming my digits over his ears and reveling in the catch of his breath.

My waistband loosens and massive digits dip into my panties. I almost succumb to the raging inferno as he cups my sex in his hand and digs his fat middle fingertip through my folds to tease my sopping entrance.

My body gasps and moans as my mind watches in a haze of horror and embarrassment as I orgasm while he removes the failed plug from my channel.

Exhaustion saps my energy away, making the high of pleasure morph into a terrifying blob of ink as the abyss returns, opening its maw and threatening to pull me into nothing. My arms flop to my sides and weight presses my lashes over my eyes.

The glorious rumble emanating from Cahress' chest changes, fury and concern leaking from his heart to mine.

"Shit. Duri, open your mouth."

Fabric rustles as I drift closer to the well of nothingness, and when my eyelids finally lift, shock jumpstarts my heart.

His cock, thick and long and every shade of blue imaginable, juts in front of my face. The hot, wild scent of him fills my mouth with saliva, but the partially inflated knot at his base and the wicked-looking knobs protruding along the top and bottom of his shaft fill me with fear.

He pries my teeth apart and wraps his fist around his shaft. My mind splinters as a drop of pearly white liquid lands on my tongue.

I could feast on him for days and never tire of his taste. Like power and joy and the salty-sweet ocean of love I sense waiting within his soul. I want more.

Pressure on my scalp prevents me from lifting my head and taking his bright blue tip into my mouth, but he gives me what I desire, even if my instincts balk at being denied. Viscous fluid shoots from his shaft, startling me enough to garnish a squeak from my chest, but basal needs demand I consume what he offers.

I swallow with my mouth open, abhorring the thought of wasting a single drop. When I can't keep up with his offering, his breathing turns ragged and his hand clamps around the base of his cock.

Life flows through my veins as my stomach warms from his seed, my cells clamoring to soak up his essence.

He releases my hair and prowls backward until his shaft rests along my labia. I gulp down the rest of his offering and close my mouth, too terrified for words and yet so ready my flesh sparks where he touches me.

"I want to thrust my hips and feel your slippery, swollen folds on my nodes. I want to take my time and sink into you so slowly you orgasm with each breath. I want to rut you so thoroughly your slick soaks us from head to toe."

His stillness opens the doors on my lust, flaring the flames into mountainous heights.

"When we're safe, I'll do all these things. When you're ready, I'll rut you so thoroughly you'll forget what it was like to ever be apart from me."

He lifts his hips, fits his cockhead to my opening, and pushes forward with a measured, controlled lowering of his body.

I split in two, my pussy in glorious agony while my brain short circuits. He changes everything I thought I knew about myself, erases every nicety society drilled into my head, and strips away every defense I built around my heart.

His invasion hurts. I stretch and stretch as he mercilessly pushes deeper and deeper into my body. I scratch and push and pull, wanting him to stop but needing his essence more with every passing millisecond.

His knobs mash against sensitive organs, stimulating nerve endings never touched before. Slick erupts from my core, splattering his groin and dripping down his clad legs.

It isn't fair. I want to see him, need to explore every inch of him, but he still wears the damn suit.

My fingernails scratch along the fabric, but it doesn't budge. Soft strands fill my fists, a vicious voice emerging from my instincts, and I'm helpless against her demands. Past the dense fur and into the skin beneath, I sink my nails into his scalp and grip his hair as though I'll die if I lose my prize.

His partially inflated knot mashes against my entrance.

He won't fit. There's no way. Little mewls and whimpers bounce off stone, confusing me until I realize they come from my own throat. Melodious and deep, his purr soothes the turmoil in my soul.

Until a savage thrust of his hips buries himself deeper than should be possible.

Chapter Fourteen

Cahress

Her silent scream satisfies my alpha instincts. With her head tossed back and her hair in disarray, she looks like a fallen goddess.

One I will happily worship for the rest of my life.

She's too tight. Too wet. Too perfect.

As she comes apart under me, my hands roam along her beautiful curves, needing to stroke and test and adore her. Her round belly presses against me, the tiny life within only adding to her beauty.

I can't wait to plant my own seed within her womb.

For now, I give her what her body so desperately needs. Once we get to safety, I'll give her what she needs *and more*. So much more.

The pulsing of her channel as I begin a slow retreat undoes me. My hips snap forward and my release burns through me so suddenly my head spins.

Lava bursts from my groin and expands my knot before scorching my shaft and shooting from my tip. Locked behind her pubic bone, my knot pulses impossibly bigger. Her tight, wet heat beckons more and more seed from me, until my spine feels hollow and my ears ring.

I want to give her more, but small sounds of distress pull me back from my mania.

Tears drench her hair and sobs wrack her chest. Fearing the worst, I roll over and cocoon her in my arms.

"Did I hurt you?"

She shakes her head against my chest but continues to cry. I grit my teeth and will my orgasms to end while threatening my knot with abstinence should it deflate too soon.

Yeah, knot, if you don't do your job, I'll leave you outside of the wondrous grip of her body next time.

Now is not the time to lose my sanity.

"What's wrong, little mama? Talk to me."

"Th-thank you."

The tight band of worry loosens from around my ribs.

"Don't thank me. You should be in a soft nest with all the comforts an omega can have, not trapped in a cave and on the run."

"I-I mean it. Thank you, Cahress. No one has ever given me so much."

I let my awe at her resilience emanate from my heart, hoping she understands just how deeply I adore her.

Her sharp inhale jerks my attention to her face. She studies her hands as though they aren't her own. I open my mouth to ask her what's wrong, but she speaks before I do.

"I made you bleed."

When I understand the meaning behind her words, I gather her wrists into my right hand and pin them to my shoulder, forcing her to stretch along my body. The shifting makes my cock jerk and spurt more seed into her.

"Sorry, little mama. We can't take the chance."

Her brows pinch in confusion while her bottom lip disappears between her teeth.

"No tasting my blood," I clarify.

"Oh, I wasn't—" she stops mid-sentence, replaying the last few seconds in her mind. Her eyes widen as she recalls her fingers inching toward her mouth.

"I'm sorry."

"Don't be. It's instinct. How do you feel?"

The blush of passion on her face deepens as embarrassment twists her features. She glances away before returning her attention to my face.

"Stretched."

I can't help but purr, her answer laced with satisfaction.

"But also… good. Very good."

Her tentative answer pulls a chuckle from me, which sends us both to groaning when she bounces around on top of me.

"Lay down and rest. I'll take care of you."

She shakes her head and answers with a small chuckle of her own.

"I can't do much else right now, can I?"

Who knew laughter could make a knot harder?

I smile ruefully at her and reach for the little bag. Pulling out a packet of wipes, I clean her dainty fingers, planting a kiss on each one before releasing her wrists.

She settles down on top of me, her arms tucked under her chest to take the pressure off her belly, and falls asleep between one breath and the next.

Satisfaction permeates through my entire being. Even the unfulfilled lifemating bond sings with joy despite the bittersweet ache in my chest.

My bare hands enjoy her curves, their touch light so as not to disturb the sleep she so badly needs. As the minutes pass and stretch into hours, the bone deep weariness I sense in her gradually eases. Each time my knot threatens to deflate, I shift and reawaken my cock. At first, I use a gentle push of my palm on her hip, but when my toes tingle and head swims from giving so much of myself to her, I grow bolder.

She sighs and turns her head to face the other direction when I run both hands up and down her back.

Her moan as I sneak my digits between her arm and torso to play with her soft breasts makes my tip jerk deep within her body. I wedge a hand under her hip and find the semi soft bundle of nerves above her opening, unable to resist teasing it into firmness.

Soft noises emit from her sleepy throat, and I can't help but let my other hand explore her ass and thighs, briefly wondering where her skirt went before slipping my hand between her legs. Bracketing our joined bodies with my fingers, I groan and pluck at her stretched folds, my hunger rising despite already being as deep within her as possible.

"Duri, wake up."

She nuzzles against my chest, adorable and enticing. I wish I could rip off my suit and feel her flesh against mine, but I can't risk being caught by the ISC.

We can't linger here much longer. At the very least, we must return to the group and figure out what the next step is.

She shakes her head when I call her name again, so I add a warning to my purr and draw a wet circle around her clit.

Dazed brown eyes shift up to me, the flush on her cheeks apparent even in the red and yellow lights.

"Hmm?"

Still not fully awake, she scrunches her brows and ekes out a noise of concern.

I draw another circle around her clit and skim my fingernails over her stretched folds. Her choked gasp lifts my lips.

"Come for me, little mama."

I flick my drenched finger over her erect bundle of nerves and grind my fingers along our joined intimates. She shatters, throwing her head back in bliss as she clamps down on my overstimulated cock.

She's perfection. The last epic wave of seed leaves me shaking and overwhelmed, searching for the strength necessary to follow through with what I must do. For a few moments, we lay without moving, listening to our ragged breathing as we recover from our orgasms.

My knot begins to deflate. I roll over, pushing the clothing under her so she doesn't touch the cold, hard stone, and snatch two things from the tiny bag of supplies. The first, a sterile packet of absorbent material, I tear open with my teeth before wrapping it around the base of my cock.

After a bit of awkward shuffling, I prop her ass higher than her shoulders, stuffing three pairs of pants under her hips just before my knot pops free from behind her pubic bone.

Using my reflexes, I yank my shaft from her and push the fabric into her channel with my fingers, barely losing any of our mixed essences. Forcing the cotton deeper, but not as far as my knot was, I open the second packet and cover her entire mound with the large pad of waterproof gauze. I lean to the side and snag surgical tape from the bag and seal everything within while touching her flesh the least amount possible.

"Hold this while I find your clothes."

Her dainty fingers tentatively take the place of my much larger ones. I find her underclothes and consider stuffing them in one of my pockets instead of sliding them onto her body.

She probably doesn't want to wear them anyway, since they're full of dried slick.

The scrap of fabric once pressed against her magnificent pussy disappears into my pocket.

Scowling at my own foolishness, but not willing to correct myself, I turn back to the small pack and search through the inventory, surprised to find clean socks, female underthings, a small shirt, and a pair of pants.

Who snuck those in, Jokur or Choku? I hold in a snort and pull the clothes out of the bottom of the pack. I must be truly addled if I ask myself such a ridiculous question—of course Jokur included the niceties. Choku wouldn't have the first clue how to pamper a female, while omegas flock to Jokur's charm.

I lift Duri's ankles one at a time and slip them through the leg holes, fascinated by her dainty feet. She jerks when I smooth a finger over her sole, a strangled sound coming from her throat.

I slide my gaze to her face, intending to gloat over having found a ticklish spot, but her expression stops me. With careful, quick motions, I pull the garment up her legs and into place before doing the same with the pants. I help brace her hips up and push the mound of fabric out from under her before wrapping my arm under her shoulders and lifting her into a seated position.

She squeezes her eyes shut for a moment before blinking rapidly, her breaths shallow and ragged as the red drains from her face.

"I'm sorry. I just got dizzy so suddenly."

Her shaky voice and wobbling breasts kill me.

"I shouldn't have left you in that position for so long. The added weight on your spine can't be good for circulation."

"I've never thought of myself as frail, but around you, I feel delicate. Fragile. Breakable."

She looks away from my eyes for the first time and blinks, a look of shock crossing her features as her arm raises to shield her naked breasts. I purr and skim my hand over her hip and up her abdomen, enjoying the firm proof of virility and life, before cupping her left breast. Her breath hitches and in a brilliant display of bravery, she lifts her arm and places her palm over my heart.

"But I've also never felt so strong or needed. Never felt so... alive. Thank you, Cahress."

My thumb skims over her firm nipple and I lean forward, desperate to take her mouth with my own. Her eyes widen and lips part, desire shimmering from her gaze.

I curse as my mask prevents me from tasting her. My forehead settles on hers, my breaths sawing in and out of my lungs like fire.

"Don't thank me yet, Duri. Wait until you're safe."

"But I am safe. At least, I feel safe when I'm with you."

Pride expands my chest, the emotion filling my lungs and expelling on a low rumble.

"You honor me, little mama, but the truth is, we aren't safe. And it kills me, but we can't stay here any longer, no matter how much I want to knot you over and over again."

She nods her understanding, even as worry tightens her brow. I grab the shirt and prepare to slide it over her head, but she stops me and points to the discarded bra.

A snarl sneaks into my purr.

"I hate thinking of your gorgeous breasts being so confined."

An entrancing blush creeps from her chest to her cheeks.

"No, I need them, Cahress. Especially if I have to run."

Her pleading eyes and embarrassment sway me. I sigh and help her into the diabolical contraption, pushing her hand away and enjoying one last caress before closing the front clasp. She lets me pull the shirt over her shoulders, shaking her head when the garment that looked so tiny in my hands hangs loose around her. The collar slips, revealing her shoulder, but she tugs it up and fixes the bottom hem. Her bellybutton creates an imprint on the gray fabric, making me want to stroke her belly.

I gather the clean socks and slip them onto her feet, noting the slight swelling in her ankles as I put her shoes on.

A few quick tugs and my cock lays trapped against my thigh by my suit. Even though I can't smell her, I don't bother to clean myself further, wanting to keep every bit of her.

She moves as though to stand, but I sweep her onto my lap and pile the used clothes together before handing her a meal packet and the water hose. Within seconds, I finish packing, donning my vest and chest harness and slinging the bag onto my back. I surge to my feet as I clip the top half of my mask into place and stand holding the most precious omega in the known galaxies, nuzzling the top of her head with my chin.

I disengage the laser grid, tuck it into my pocket, and toss a time delay match into the pile of clothes before stalking to the room where my teammates should be.

No laser grid blocks the opening. No sounds come from the pitch-black cave.

I hurry past the eerily empty room and tuck Duri closer to my chest while silently pulling my blade from its holster.

Her muscles tense as she senses my alertness. She knows as well as I do that something's wrong.

Daylight shines through the cracks in the outer door, but I keep my steady pace and sharpen my senses.

Dread settles into my guts with every step.

Chapter Fifteen

Duri

His lithe movements hold an air of expected violence. I don't want to leave his arms, but how can he protect us if he's holding me?

"Put me down."

My whisper barely reaches my own ears, fear making me too cautious to speak any louder.

He stops next to the exit and presses his back to the cave wall as he lowers his covered mouth to my ear.

"No. Press the top button in my right earpiece."

My fingers shake, but I do what he says with relative ease, holding my breath in fear and expectation.

I resign myself to doing anything he says the moment he says it. He truly knows best, and to think I understand anything about this world would be folly.

Silence stretches on until my nerves feel on the verge of snapping from waiting. Bright blue orbs meet mine, his expression fierce. When he tilts his head so his ear leans toward me, I reach up and click the same button. He turns and murmurs quietly to me as he stalks back into the darkness.

"They intercepted communication from an unknown convoy, so they moved to a different tunnel. We shouldn't go out in the daylight, so we'll bunker down again and wait until—"

He stops mid-sentence and lunges into a sprint. I can't see anything in the dark, but he runs through the maze of corridors as though evil pursues us.

The hairs stand up on my nape. I strain my ears and hear a distant scuffing of boots, the sound faint as though the person tries to be stealthy.

Thankful for his acute senses, I cling to him as he weaves deeper into the cave system, carrying me away from the sounds of men's whispers and the quiet rustle of gear against large bodies.

Darting into a tunnel so narrow he has to turn sideways and shuffle down it, he angles me closer to him so I don't scrape along the wall and whispers words I can't hear through the pounding of my heart.

Tense minutes pass as he continues deeper into the maze until I've lost all sense of direction. When nothing but the gentle current of air from Cahress' swift movement fills the air, I force my muscles to relax and regulate my breathing in hopes of calming my racing heart.

An agonized, furious curse pierces my calm.

"Little mama, listen to me."

He sets me on my feet. I wobble in confusion and grab onto his arm for balance.

"Run."

He turns me and presses his front against my back, giving my shoulders a quick squeeze and nuzzling my head for a split second before threading the water sack straps onto my arms. He wraps his thick fingers around my right wrist and places my palm on the wall.

"Stay to the right. Keep going, as fast as you can, but be careful. Don't trip. Don't look back. Just run."

"B-but."

"Go, Duri. Now."

I don't want to. Gods, how I hate the strain in his voice, but my feet follow his command. The urgency ringing from his words gives strength to my shaking legs, and after a few steps, my heels strike with a steady yet tentative rhythm.

The darkness keeps me cautious. Unable to see, I hold my left arm straight out in front of me and run my right hand along the wall.

Masculine voices call out, but the rocks echo the sounds, warping them until I can't tell if they're right behind me or miles away. Tears stream down my face as the tape holding the sanitary pad in place comes loose and wetness leaks down my leg.

I stumble through the darkness, terrified of what's ahead and horrified of what could be behind me. Ice forms in my spine and slowly solidifies my veins until I shiver from the cold and struggle to continue forward.

Shouts give way to screaming. The sounds of fighting morph to gurgles and death. Weapons discharge, blasting thunder through the caves.

I can't stop stumbling forward. Each step seems to take a millennium. My soul ages as the outcome of the war raging behind me seems unfavorable.

Louder than the boom from the firearms, a masculine roar freezes me in place.

They hurt Cahress. I pivot on my heels, terror unlike anything I've ever known urging me to race back the way I came. He needs help. I'm the only one around to give it.

Strong arms wrap around me from behind as a massive, gloved palm clamps down over the entire bottom half of my face.

I lose it. A wild beast takes over my body, flailing and biting and scratching. When my lungs threaten to burst and a fresh wave of fluids runs down my thighs, I scream into the hand covering my mouth and drop into sanity, realizing the futility of my actions.

My arms curl around my abdomen to protect the most precious gift in the universe.

"Hush, tiny female. I'm Choku, Cahress' teammate. Come with me."

He pulls me backward, not giving me a chance to refuse. My head shakes and rubs his hand against my face, filling my eyes with tears as the sensation reminds me too much of Cahress' gloved digits.

He lifts his palm just enough to allow me to whisper.

"No! You must go help him."

"I will, but not until you're back with the group. Cahress would kill me if I left you here alone."

I nod, eager to do anything to get this gigantic male to aid my alpha, seeing how irrational it was for me to turn back toward the fight. He sent me away to protect me. I have zero fighting skills and would only be putting my daughter in danger.

Choku lifts me off my feet and cradles me against his chest. Even though his suit blocks his scent, every cell within my body balks at being held by a strange alpha, but I remain as still as possible so I don't hinder him.

With my sense of time already skewed, I have no idea how long it takes to be blinded by the sun, but I blink away my confusion and try to focus on our surroundings.

The building carved into stone whizzes by too quickly. Orange and pink, the colors of sunrise, fill the narrow expanse of sky visible between the canyon walls. I turn and view my protector for the first time. My breath catches in my throat as eyes devoid of pupils and flesh blacker than night peer from a mask identical to my alpha's. Yanking my attention away from the intricate patterns within his eyes, I realize they mimic the view of galaxies in space, like tiny specks of light dancing within a void.

He banks so quickly I tense, fearful of falling, but his sure strides keep us moving forward.

It's taking too long. He needs to get back to Cahress. Now.

He darts around another corner and halts without warning, placing me on my feet on a patch of sand. My head spins and knees threaten to give out, but he holds onto my shoulders until I have my balance before he steps back. Gloved digits point to a boulder on the right.

Commander Ru'en steps from behind the covering and nods. When I turn around, nothing lingers of Choku's presence.

"Are you hurt?"

My attention snaps to Commander Ru'en, his cold tone at odds with the question. I shake my head. He stalks toward me. I shift to step backward, but he lifts me into his arms before I can protest.

Frigid air emanates from his suit, chilling my flesh.

Wet warmth leaks from my core, and as he carries me in the direction he came from, I realize I stood with one arm wrapped under my belly and the other between my legs, trying to hold in Cahress' essence. I no doubt looked obscene and pathetic.

Too frazzled to worry about this cruel-looking alpha's perception of me, I keep my hand plastered against the crotch of my pants, desperate to keep every drop of my alpha's potent seed within me.

His rolling stride carries us around the boulder and up a steep incline. I cringe several times despite how easily he climbs the hidden path, since the loose pebbles and cliff on our right makes the way seem so perilous. Higher and higher he climbs, traversing the distance faster than should be possible.

The rocks under his boots level out as he steps over the ridge of the canyon wall, revealing a wide expanse of sky and dead earth. Dry and brittle, the land in front of us carries its own sense of danger and malice, different from the maze of stone and yet just as deadly.

He doesn't pause, merely powers into the hot wind like a creature possessed.

With his icy figure pressed against me, my senses reel at the play of hot and cold, the chapped skin on my face hurting from the extremes. Off in the distance, tiny figures stumble through the harsh conditions. The closer we get, the larger some grow, while others remain low to the ground, and when I recognize Thret's bony plates, my brain snaps into focus.

The smaller figures are the omegas, while the taller ones are Cahress' teammates.

Only three female forms struggle over the cracked, dry ground. My clit pulses as I press my hand too tightly against my folds, my panic instinctively tightening my grip, but I calm as I find the missing omegas.

Each alpha carries an omega in their arms and another on their back, with Thret carrying both the mother and boy together against his chest. Those four, the three motivating each other to continue, and myself account for all eight omegas from the original group.

My heart cries for the male who showed me such amazing care, because if it weren't for him, I wouldn't still be alive.

I need for him to be safe. I need him. My child needs him. I tell myself he can't have been the creature to make such a horrendous, pain-filled sound as I stumbled through the darkness, but no amount of lying changes the knowledge deep in my bones.

Cahress isn't fine. He's hurt and in trouble.

All because he tried to protect me.

Chapter Sixteen

Cahress

P ain sears through my side with every breath, but I fight the inky void of unconsciousness and focus on the lackeys surrounding me. Blood drips and congeals from my mangled suit, the combination of their knife and high voltage weapons proving more than I bargained for.

They made no more sound than five soldiers. Yet here I stand, surrounded by six dead bodies and a dozen foes hell bent on subduing me.

I dodge another swing of a stun rod and jab my blade into the connected forearm, twisting the knife and yanking upward to extract my last handheld weapon. Four alphas rush forward, attacking my legs and torso. With a vicious roar, I grab the nearest body part and pull, simultaneously flinging my knife at the asshole to my left.

If they were trying to kill me, I'd be dead by now. I rushed into their trap, needing to stop their pursuit and give Duri a chance to escape, not expecting so many of them to be hiding within the larger cavern, and so my current situation is my own fault.

My right leg gives out as a baton cracks against the back of my knee, but my fist connects with the idiot who got close enough for me to grab his throat despite my beginning descent.

I earn another long gash along my upper back and a kick to my injured ribs as I punch the male again and again until blood pours from his head. Agony blasts across my senses as they continue their assault, hitting and kicking me from all directions.

Three high voltage weapons press into me at the same time, frying my senses and singeing every hair follicle on my body. Reality becomes a faint echo of truth, blocked from my brain by death as my heart refuses to beat. All traces of energy flee as though sucked loose by the currents of electricity.

My fractured ribs crack again as brutal hands pump against my sternum, jumpstarting my stalled heart and forcing my mind back into the present.

Metal chains clink around me, pulling so tight my fingers and toes ache from the lack of circulation.

I relax my body, only partly feigning unconsciousness, biding my time as I gather my senses.

It takes much too long. By the time I no longer flicker between barely clinging to the present and swimming in blinding pain, straps hold my cocooned body to a board and four alphas carry me into the light of dusk.

They hoist me into the back of a transporter and rap on the wall between the cargo bay and the driver. Before they even finish strapping my board to the floor, the vehicle bumps over the rough terrain. A meaty, gloved hand rips away my mask and replaces it with their own shoddy version, the filtering system allowing a trace of the surrounding scents in my nostrils. He drops a cloth over my head, blindfolding me.

Agony spears into my chest and back as the craft jolts and accelerates.

All I can do is count the minutes as they pass and pray my little mama made it to relative safety. I take her absence as a good sign—either I distracted the soldiers well enough for her to find a hiding place or one of my teammates intercepted her.

Minutes become an hour. An hour morphs to two. Blood congeals around the shallow gashes on my upper back, but the piercing pain in my ribs worsens. The line leading from my soul pulses with misery as the distance between myself and my lifemate grows.

When the vibrations on the hull of the vehicle change, I suck down a quick breath, waking myself with the slicing pain in preparation of whatever comes next. The engine slows but the sound bounces back louder, telling me we've entered an enclosed space.

A few unfavorable words from my captors precede the jostling of the board under me as they lift me from the floor, timing it so that the moment the transport rolls to a stop they jump out with me in tow.

Familiar scents fill my nostrils, the tangy bite of disinfectant with an underlying sweetness of death and misery the perfume I associate with ISC facilities.

I cannot fear for myself. I will not allow it, yet dread builds behind my sternum.

The board stops bucking under me half a millisecond before I free fall a few inches, slamming into a raised platform with a loud smack. My ears ring and my entire body sings in pain, but I squint up through bright fluorescent lights and snarl at the reflective masks hovering over me as gloved fingers snatch the cloth from my face.

Five personnel scurry about, rolling machines and talking in rapid succession while four guards stand with their hands poised over their weapons, their watchful eyes alerting me of their readiness. I relax as best I can while staying alert and snarl as the white clad personnel descend.

A buzzing razor clears a patch of fur from my arm, the shaver struggling to handle my dense undercoat. A needle sinks into my vein and extracts several vials of crimson. I tense, prepared to fight should they try to insert any kind of substance into my bloodstream, but to my surprise, they merely slide the needle free and cover my arm with a bandage before winding a thick collar around my neck. Tiny pinpricks on either side of my jugulars yanks a hiss from me, but the width of the collar prevents me from lifting my head and biting the slim fingers as they retreat.

A guard grabs the platform near my head and pushes, gliding what must be an operating table or gurney into the hall on silent wheels. Large fluorescent lights stripe up my vision while the four alphas dressed in black surround me.

The sound of water dripping onto tile enrages me on a purely instinctual level. I vibrate with the need to rampage free of my chains, but a door bangs open and closed several times before the snick of a lock sounds.

Other males, smelling of blood and fear, shuffle their bare feet on tile and wheeze like men grappling to hang on to their sanity.

A faucet turns on somewhere, the rush of water almost drowning out the harsh commands of other ISC enforcers.

Chains clink as a black clad idiot removes the loop nearest my wrists. He snaps black bands around them and snaps a coated rope between them.

A zap of electricity runs from my wrists to my throat and back, tightening every muscle in between.

"You break the connection between the wrist cuffs, and a shock four times stronger will begin and won't stop until they're connected again. Got it, freak?"

I glare at him, daring him to release me and find out my response. He scoffs and slaps more bands around my ankles after slicing my boots off my feet and jerking my socks free with hate-filled hands.

An alpha wearing a white hazmat suit steps into the circle of black guards, scans me from head to toe, then turns to the moron near my feet.

"Hurry up and get Subject 852 ready. They're waiting for him."

Without waiting for a response, he shifts his reflective mask toward my legs and torso, no doubt studying the thick pelt of tan and brown sticking out from my sliced and torn suit.

"Triple the water pressure for Subject 852, otherwise we might not clean through all layers of fur."

Black gloves descend in unison, following some unspoken cue between my four original captors. They strip me of all chains except a tight band around my chest and thighs, stand me on my feet, cut my clothes from me, hobble my ankles together and add a rope behind my back, creating a completed loop around my torso from my wrists.

Cruel hands push me forward, almost sending me to the white tiled floor, but my reflexes shuffle my feet and save my balance.

A line of broken looking alphas stand with their shoulders hunched and their sides pressed against the wall. Their bruised and bleeding flesh stands out amidst the all-encompassing white of the room.

A tall, lanky alpha with a massive welt on his left temple jerks his attention to me. I watch as the light brown of his irises, so similar to the rich color of Duri's, morphs to black as his pupils expand.

His striking features fill with fury so potent my own vision takes on a red tinge.

"You! What did you do?" Sharp white teeth glint as he gnashes them at me, stepping toward me.

"Subject 839, return to position."

He ignores the command, turning his naked body square with mine.

"You smell of her! I'll kill you!"

Adrenaline floods my system, making my muscles bulge and senses heighten. As he lunges toward me, I drop my shoulder and jerk my hands to my collar.

Despite his enraged state, he flicks his eyes at the guard beside me in clear communication.

Duri's scent on my cock may have sent him into rampage, but he isn't so far gone he's forgotten who the true enemy is.

The rope stretches across my back and snaps as I rip the collar from my throat. A hum sounds as I wrench the bands from my wrists, a jolt of electricity running up my legs before I tear the cuffs off my ankles.

I move just in time to grab the incoming baton, my swiftness yanking it from gloved digits and burying it into the closest alpha's gut before I swing it upward. Bones shatter as it smacks against his forearm.

Another weapon aims for my head, their patience gone. No longer do they attempt to subdue me—they strike for areas intended to kill.

Violence breaks out, only a few forms remaining huddled against the wall. In the mayhem, I steal another baton and toss it to an alpha straddling the white suit who held the massive water hose, his blows cracking the reflective shield over the enforcer's head. I intercept a stun weapon and strong arm the tip into the black suit's neck, hitting the flesh between his mask and his suit. His other hand grabs at my mask, but I ruin his last-ditch effort to save himself by jerking my head to the side and breaking the strap. I press his own finger over the trigger. He seizes and keeps on seizing, his digit clamping down and creating a closed circuit.

The last two black clad guards swing at me, one aiming for my temple while the other swings for my lower back. As I dodge and jab my fist upward into my enemy's groin, a whiff of the sweetest, purest perfume invades my nostrils. My cock hardens so fast my head spins, but I follow through on my punch and pivot on the balls of my feet, sweeping the alpha unfortunate enough to bear the brunt of my fist feet out from under him.

He crashes to the ground a few seconds before my last assailant crumples to the floor under the weight of enraged alphas.

Squaring my shoulders and straightening my spine, I ignore the pulsing of my shaft as it juts into the frigid air and take stock of the situation. Either dead or unconscious, nine ISC personnel lay sprawled on the floor while fifteen alphas, not including myself, stand naked, battered, and so high on bloodlust feral growls bounce off the walls.

An intricate plan won't work. My training may allow me access to logical thought, but most of these other captives lack the cunning lethality of a warrior.

They'll all fight anyway, except for the two still huddled against the wall. They both cower as though they expect to be struck at any time.

I don't know how deep in the facility we are, but we have an advantage we'll never get again, so I snarl, drawing all battle-ready eyes to mine.

"Where's Duri? What did you do to her?" I turn to the tall and thin alpha who began the attack and answer him.

"I helped her. I protected her."

"She's safe?"

"No."

"She's here?!"

"I fucking hope not. She's my lifemate."

Silence as surprise lifts his brows gives me time to continue.

"I'm Cahress. You're Seung, my omega's best friend. And we're all getting out of here. Follow me. Stay together. Collect any weapons you come across. We'll never have a chance like this again."

Chapter Seventeen

Duri

White pupils grow as Commander Ru'en steps into the shade of a decrepit building. With only half a roof and three remaining walls, the ruins provide little relief from the blaring sun and incessant wind, but I welcome the change all the same. My skin feels shriveled and burnt despite my attempts at shielding myself from the sun. Mounds of sand pile under the window and gather in the corners of the old room, making the space even smaller.

Commander Ru'en sets me on my feet for the first time in several hours. My legs shake too much to remain standing for long, so I shuffle forward and accept Henna's help in lowering my body down next to hers. We huddle in a tight group as the alphas gather where the fourth wall would be if it remained standing. They speak in voices too low to hear over the howling wind, even with the pitiful excuse for a structure blocking the worst of the blast.

We pass the water sacks around in relative silence, too worn out to talk.

My heart aches worse than my body does, the steady thumping threatening to shred the stretched link connecting my soul to my alpha's. Even though we haven't claimed each other, the most basic part of me shrieks and wails over the distance between us. I need and want him by my side.

Sand sticks to my pants, clinging to the last traces of wetness seeping from my core. If it weren't for the threat of dehydration, I'd release the tension behind my eyes, but I can't risk putting my child in more danger. I take a few sips of water and pass the hose to Henna, using the tepid liquid to center my thoughts.

My ears pick up the sound of a vehicle. It moves toward us so fast the engine roars. I snap my attention to the three alphas standing at the only plausible way out, knowing my weakened state won't allow me to climb up the steep mound of sand to escape out the window.

Alert but not alarmed, the alphas don't move to evade the incoming vehicle.

Uneasy hope sweeps through the group.

Commander Ru'en steps forward and waves the transporter to park in front of the building. He walks to the driver's window and converses with the human behind the wheel before stalking back to us.

"Get in. We can't head straight to base, but there's supplies to last us a few days in case we can't shake the ISC scouts."

Henna struggles to her feet and speaks, her voice shaky with exhaustion and fear.

"They're still following us?"

"Yes, otherwise I wouldn't have risked putting out an emergency beacon so soon after our last correspondence. Get everyone in the cargo bay. Now."

His menacing snarl motivates everyone to jump to their feet, but I rise to my knees and fight a wave of dizziness. Everything hurts. Nothing makes sense.

The sky, so painfully bright, flickers between the yellow of the sun and the white of fluorescent bulbs. My ears send me the howling wind, but my chest constricts with the sound of violence.

A thrill of victory runs up my spine, pulling my eyebrows together in confusion. Henna loops her arm under mine to help me up, but I stay as I am except to turn my gaze to Commander Ru'en.

Whatever he sees in my expression ratchets him to full alert, an almost visible field of awareness popping up around him as he steps closer.

"What is it, omega?"

"Something changed. Cahress..."

Frigid hands lift me from the ground and carry me into the transporter. He sets me on the bench and crouches in front of me.

"Did he mark you? Did you mark him?"

For once, his white pupils and black irises don't frighten me. The savage and gleeful emotions exploding through my chest don't belong to me, but I experience them as my own.

"No, but I feel him. He's fighting. He's *winning*."

The world around me fractures and mends itself. A tiny limb flutters against my ribs. Certainty fills me.

I can help him this time. I can find him.

"That way. He's that way."

With my eyes closed and one hand resting on my belly, I extend my other arm and point where instincts demand I go.

Commander Ru'en doesn't ask any questions, merely curses under his breath and bangs on the tiny window between the cab and the back. The piece of glass slides open with a metallic clank as the vehicle begins moving.

"New intel. We're going that way. Standby for updates."

I open my eyes to find him turning toward me, one hand up to his ear. When my brain decides to work, I realize he's talking into his suit's communicator.

"Request all nearby units to my beacon. Possible new ISC facility located. One Warrior Elite inside. Status unknown."

His last two words ring ominously through the cramped space, but my heart declares them as false.

I know Cahress' status. He's deep in the throes of rampage, reveling in the pain he doles out and triumphant in his violence.

Sand plumes behind the vehicle as the engine whines. I occasionally point when the direction changes, clueless to everything except the urge to find the male who stole the better part of my soul. A masculine voice says something in a commanding tone, but I can't force my mind to single out the individual words, so I ignore whoever spoke.

Gentle hands, much too small to be an alpha's, touch my shoulder and glide across my front, buckling me into the seat.

The terrain becomes so rough the back of my skull cracks against the wall twice before the driver slows down. I mentally urge him to move faster, but my battered body prefers the smoother ride.

When the driver weaves this way and that, I force my eyes to the back opening and note the barren mountains stretching along our left flank, forcing him to dodge boulders too big to drive over.

A vicious tug on the link prompts my finger to shift deeper into the mountain range. Commander Ru'en shouts. The vehicle changes course.

Every cell in my body vibrates. The delicate life in my womb jerks and flips. Eagerness has me sitting forward, pressing the seatbelt harder against my sternum.

The transporter swings around a sharp corner so fast the rear tires skid sideways before gaining traction and propelling us forward.

A masculine voice yells from the rooftop. I look at my surroundings for the first time and realize Commander Ru'en is the only male within the cargo bay, so the other two teammates must be on the roof, since both seats in the front were taken before we embarked. Another harsh word filters down from the ceiling, prompting a response from Commander Ru'en.

A massive form drops down to block my view of the mountains. Thret stands on the tailgate with one hand grasping the lip of the roof as he pulls a weapon from his belt.

"We're too close. Jokur and I will—"

The female in the passenger seat, whose beta scent stands out amidst the omegas, shouts, alarm making her sound angry.

The vehicle screeches to a halt. My fingers ache from holding on to the edge of my seat, but I train my focus on the tiny window at the front in hopes of seeing what made them stop. Light shines onto the side of my face as Thret jumps free of the vehicle and disappears around the side.

Gears grind as the driver shifts to reverse and mashes the gas. He turns the wheel so sharply every omega within the cargo bay gasps and grabs on to whatever they can, the sudden change in momentum making my seatbelt dig into my skin. I move my hands and wedge my thumbs under the lap belt, easing the tension from my protruding belly.

A loud pop yanks my attention to the rear, and I glimpse a large, round metal door sunk into the side of the mountain. As it swings outward, Commander Ru'en steps into my line of sight.

Cahress is there. Right there, within sight, if the behemoth would move his butt out of my way.

My weight shifts again as the vehicle lurches to a stop, the driver shifting into drive and stomping on the gas as quickly as possible. Commander Ru'en grabs the roof, opening a sliver of space between his side and the wall. I lean, desperate to see what's beyond.

Naked flesh shines in the bright light of the sun, a group of alphas emerging from the smoke-filled tunnel. Front and center, Cahress stalks toward us, so close I can see his blown pupils. With big round eyes, small otter-like round ears, and a triangular nose, the thick golden mustache and beard framing his mouth accentuate his full, sensual lips. My eyes follow the line of his long, thick neck and my mouth waters at the exposed flesh of his chest and the trail of hairless skin arrowing down his abdominals.

Bigger than any creature has a right to be, his wide shoulders, tapered torso, and thick legs sport more muscles than should be possible. A thick undercoat of sandy brown fur peaks out from a darker shade of brown along his limbs. I blink as golden strands hidden within the layered coat reflect the sunlight back at me.

I want to sink my fingers into his fur and feel his hard muscles under my touch.

Jutting from his groin, his turgid cock bobs with every step, stealing my breath and flooding me with yearning.

He's mesmerizing.

And needy.

I want to sate his needs, just like how he sated mine.

The vehicle picks up speed, pulling away from Cahress. His expression darkens as his nostrils flare and his eyes narrow to mine.

His lips move. I can't hear him above the roar of the engine, but I feel his singular word deep in my bones.

Mine.

Yes. Yes, I'm his. My hands move on their own, releasing the buckle of my seatbelt. I grab the edge of the seat and shift my weight to stand.

"No."

Commander Ru'en's heavy hand lands on my shoulder, pushing me back against the bench.

Cahress' roar pierces my eardrums. His fury infects my chest, adding to my own frustration.

"Let me go!"

"No."

I slap his forearm, but he doesn't budge.

"Let me go!"

I hardly recognize my own voice, the vehemence and madness twisting my vocal cords until I sound unhinged.

"If I do, he'll knot you right there on the rocks. Do you think you'll survive? Because it won't just be him interested in your scent."

His words pour ice water down my spine. I bite back a cry and fumble through the motions of buckling myself back in. By the time I raise my gaze above the tailgate, tears stream down my face, wasting precious resources.

Intense yearning and simmering lust swirl through my body, but I grip my lap belt in my fists and grit my teeth, hating what I must do.

Cahress runs barefoot after us, his stormy expression a direct reflection of the pain in my heart. Knowing he won't hear me, I mouth the words my soul chants.

I love you.

The vehicle swings around the sharp curve and speeds up, weaving back through the bumpy mountain pass and blocking my view of my alpha.

As he powers through the corner, a dark shape leaps from above and lands directly on him, but instead of crumpling to the ground, he grapples with the figure. Another joins in, sliding around the corner and lunging at my lifemate.

I almost reach for my buckle again, wanting to help him, but Commander Ru'en growls a warning as I recognize the shapes as Thret and Jokur.

My adrenaline drains from me as though someone pulled a plug out of my toes, but the transporter jolts so violently I tense my muscles so I don't knock my head against the wall again.

I try to console myself by closing my eyes and turning my attention to the connection between myself and Cahress but find too much turmoil in the link. Blinking down at my lap, I soothe myself by drawing slow circles over my rounded belly, leaving one hand tight on the seatbelt to prevent it from pinching my waist.

The agitation behind my sternum eases with each breath, as though my lifemate seeks confirmation of my wellness and feeds off the serenity I find in the delicate life occupying my womb.

I sink into peace, noticing the hollow feeling in my bones for the first time since Choku carried me from the cave. A disconcerting emptiness gnaws at my insides, like a hungry beast who tasted the sweet nectar of life but was denied enough sustenance to last them until their next meal.

No, I can wait. If what Cahress gave me before was only a slice of what he can offer me and my babe, then I'll eagerly wait for another round of rutting. I relax my neck, wincing when my sore head bumps against the wall, and focus on projecting my newfound fortitude to my alpha.

I have support and supplies. He's out in the wilderness, naked, feral, and injured. If he has any chance of survival, he needs his logical mind to work, so I pour my attention into calming us down.

It works too well. I fall asleep before I finish my next breath.

Dreams of a massive, burly alpha with pale blue eyes and a devilish smirk invade my slumber, and I relish every moment he teases me.

Chapter Eighteen

Cahress

I wait for another blow, but it doesn't come. With my limbs pinned down and a heavy-as-hell alpha sitting on my stomach, I wait for my next opportunity to fight.

We didn't break free just to be captured and dragged back into the pit of hell.

My fellow naked alphas fall silent, their snarls ceasing when Choku makes his presence known. As his figure distorts and returns to his singular form, my rage abates enough for me to recognize the heavyweight sitting on me. Thret and his bony plates pin me to the sharp rocks, my pelt preventing me from turning into a pincushion.

"Get off me."

"I see you finally woke up. Anything in there, hothead?" Thret raps his knuckles against the top of my skull, not enough to hurt despite the abrasion on my forehead from a run in with a riot shield. My small round ears flatten against my head.

"Damn, not even going to ask me if I'm okay? How about a kiss, since you've already mounted me?"

Thret's expression darkens, and he smacks my skull again, the swing buffered by my short, dense hair. He rises to his feet and glares at me as he moves to my left side, opposite Jokur.

Several seconds tick by with only the wind whistling through the valley.

"Are we done with the glamour contest? We need to move," Choku rumbles from the outskirts of the group.

I sit up, aware of my injuries for the first time since I was attacked. Sore muscles, bruises, and a few abrasions, but nothing serious. Even the sense of exhaustion caused by being electrocuted fades under the peace flowing through my soul.

"I'm going after that transporter."

"No, you aren't," Thret quips.

I stand and bare my teeth at him, rolling my shoulders and preparing for a fight.

"Quit thinking with your cock and let some blood flow to your brain. They stopped you for a reason."

Choku speaks as he walks toward me, the naked alphas creating a path for him. He hands a sleeve of No Smells to the nearest male mid-stride, never breaking eye contact with me.

"She's in a vehicle full of omegas. You're in a pack of naked, feral alphas. Get your shit together, jackass."

The full scale of what might have happened hits me in the gut so hard I struggle to draw a full breath. When I finally ease my abdominals and suck in oxygen, beautiful, enticing pheromones fill my nostrils.

I lunge.

Flesh connects with black material. Choku accepts my first punch, his speckled eyes unchanging despite the power behind my fist, but he catches my follow up swing, encompassing my knuckles with his palm and wrapping his fingers over my hand.

"You smell of her!"

My snarl cuts through the howling wind and hurts my throat with its ferocity.

"I do. I carried her from the cave."

This close to him, another distinct smell assaults my senses. The same aroma wafts from my groin, sweet and pungent and much too delicious, but this scent holds an edge of despair. Salty tears mingle within the mixture of sweat, slick, and seed.

"Fuck, the plug didn't work, did it?"

Choku drops my hand and shakes his head.

Curses flow from my mouth and I bury my fingers in my hair and pull, needing the pain to prevent myself from flying into another rampage.

How can she offer me such serenity when she's in so much trouble? Nearly rutted in front of a group of raging alphas. Running from the ISC for days. Been denied the most basic life requirements. Trekked through sand and sun and rock and darkness.

She's at the end of her strength, despite my attempt to give her the seed her babe needs. Even after I knotted her in the cave, her stamina wasn't what it should be for an omega with child, the travel and harsh conditions too much for her.

She depended on that plug working. Failure means her offspring turning to its only source of nutrition—her.

"You're talking about Duri, aren't you? Where is she?"

Seung's voice breaks through my downward spiral. I straighten and meet his gaze, noting the blood dripping from his elbow.

"In the transport we saw a few moments ago."

His eyes widen and feet move the direction the vehicle disappeared, but the movement isn't conscious, merely his instincts compelling him to find the omega he impregnated.

He opens his mouth to respond, his features twisted in fury and fear, but Jokur interrupts with a sigh.

"Are we just going to stand out here in broad daylight, dicks literally swinging, until company shows up? C'mon, let's get out of here. We'll patch up injuries along the way."

After a calming breath and a glance at the imposing terrain, Seung nods, indicating his intent to continue our conversation later.

I accept a No Smell from Choku, peeling the paper backing off and slapping the white strip of fabric under my nose. My thick mustache and thicker whiskers make it brush across my nostrils, but it does its job well enough—the tempting scent of feminine juices dissipates from my senses.

Thret leads the way into the mountains, tossing a first aid pouch over his shoulder. I catch it and clean the gash on Seung's bicep before wrapping it tight enough to prevent it from bleeding so freely.

Jokur joins the group about halfway in, checking each male for injury before falling back to the next one. I do the same, checking the sun's position often. It may be hot now, but these humans don't have a pelt to keep them warm when night comes.

About an hour after we begin our march, we reach the end of the canyon. On a wandering path a few stories higher than the valley floor, the view of the land beyond the imposing stacks of rocks sends streaks of awe and dread through me. Every other step, I flick my gaze to the landscape, measuring the strip of dried, cracked land before the planet seems to sink in on itself. On the other side of the cliff, which almost stretches across the entire horizon, mounds of sand lay striated across the surface of the planet.

I catch the rumble of an engine in the distance, but see no vehicle across the expanse of flat dead zone, so I turn my attention to the mountains.

The sound teases the edge of my senses for over an hour before Thret weaves us deeper into the mountain range. A vehicle slows to a roll about ten feet below our narrow ledge, the engine dropping to a hum as the driver shifts to neutral.

Thret jumps and lands on the roof with ease before moving to the back end and dropping to one knee. He motions for Seung to follow.

After a brief hesitation, he does. He hits with a grunt, crumpling to his knees and sliding sideways. Before he reaches the edge of the roof, Thret hauls him back and drops him onto the tailgate.

The next alpha jumps, landing in a crouch and stumbling his way to the back before Seung disappears inside the cargo bay.

One by one, each alpha streaks through the air, loose hair streaming and bare limbs flailing. When only myself, Jokur, and Choku remain on the ledge, I hop down and stride to the back, swinging into the cargo bay with ease.

Most alphas already don mismatched clothes, so when the male who I tossed the first baton to offers me a folded stack of fabric, I take it. After pulling on the shorts, I give the shirt to someone else, knowing they need it more than I do.

I settle on the bench, closest to the tailgate, and hold in my unhappy grumbles as each bump in the terrain taps my head on the roof. An uneasy quiet settles over the truck, the occupants suffering through adrenaline withdrawals and uncertainty over the future.

After a long blink and steady stare, Seung dips his chin at me and rests his head against the wall, his eyes closing and posture reeking of exhaustion.

The rest of the trip passes in silence.

Mountains fade into the distance. The sun sinks below the horizon. Sand dunes block out the stars.

All the while, a profound peace flows through my soul, wicking away my discomforts and filling me with joy. I replay the last few moments before the transporter sped off, taking my little mama with it.

Her rich brown eyes shimmered with tears and her lips formed a phrase I never thought I'd hear from a female other than my mother and sisters.

I love you.

I trace the letters in my mind's eye and echo them back to her, expecting a change in the link between us, but the stream of tranquility continues to flow into me. I take and take until I overflow, soaking up every bit of her I can.

When I push the excess toward her, it ricochets back into my chest, unable to work against the current she aims at me.

Understanding fills me with dread, a wriggling mass of fear opening my eyes and turning my gaze to Seung, instinctually searching for someone who could potentially reach her.

His head lifts and bleary brown orbs dart to mine.

"What?"

"Can you feel her?"

He looks confused by my question, but he scrunches his thin brows and shakes his head. My words emerge rough and full of emotions I can't name.

"She has to stop. She's giving too much."

"What do you mean?"

My hand lifts to my chest and digs my fingernails into the skin over my heart. His tilted eyes widen as the motion conveys more than any words ever could.

"We need to hurry," he says, shooting to his feet and stumbling to the tailgate. I sit clutching my chest, focusing my attention on the incomplete bond, stretching and reaching, trying to break through the flood of feminine peace as Seung calls to my teammates.

I lose track of time, fear taking root in my swamped soul as the waves of love pouring from my omega ebb.

The tailgate bangs open.

"Where is she?" I snarl at the first creature unfortunate enough to cross my path. Director Icarr, as composed as ever, stands with her feet shoulder width apart and her identification card hanging in plain sight. She doesn't flinch, meeting my eyes with too much self-possession for my frazzled state.

"She's waiting for you, but you can't go to her until you're cleared."

Impatience yanks a growl from my chest.

"Don't argue with her. Get checked, for her safety," Commander Ru'en says, stepping around the side of the vehicle and flicking his white pupils my way before addressing the other alphas.

"You'll all be in quarantine until we're sure you won't infect us with anything."

I ignore him, turning my focus back on the small beta woman.

"Start. Now."

With a nod, she turns and motions for me to follow her, leading me into the only tent nearby.

It wasn't here when I left base camp. They must have set up a separate section within the base to check and house these new arrivals. Anyone exposed to ISC facilities must go through a full physical and observation period before they can join the regular population.

As she takes my vitals and hooks me up to machines, I try to keep my calm.

"How is she?"

Concern ghosts across her features, but she doesn't pause in her task.

"She was almost catatonic when she arrived, but we gave her fluids, vitamins, and calories intravenously and she perked up."

"Where is she now?"

"I'll take you to her as soon as I'm done."

"Where is she?"

"In a couples tent on the other side of the hill. It's fully stocked, so you'll have everything you need for the next few days."

"Does it have proper nesting materials?"

The slightest hesitation as she removes the blood pressure cuff from my arm has every muscle in my body tensing.

"Yes, but she refuses to build a nest. Or shower. Or eat."

I snarl, rip the needle out of her hand, and drop it onto the counter.

"Take me to her. Now."

Director Icarr studies me for a moment, checking the machines and weighing her options.

She nods and walks out of the tent without a word.

I follow tight on her heels.

Chapter Nineteen

Duri

I don't know where the blanket came from, but I don't have the will to tuck it tighter around me. The room seems colder than before, but I don't care. Only one thing matters.

He's still alive. Still on his way. Still needs my help.

Everything will be fine once he gets here. He has everything me and my daughter need to survive.

I dig deeper into my happiness and send it through the bond, pushing away my frustration when the act proves difficult.

He doesn't need my woes. He needs my peace and assurance.

Mended and Marked

A zipper grinds open and air tussles my hair, but my muscles refuse to roll over to see who's standing in the doorway. The bare mattress under my cheek covers a portion of my vision while the tan tent wall fills the rest, but after a slow blink, I close my eyes again and force more of myself into the bond.

Warm arms slide between the bed and my side and scoop me up to cradle me against a muscular chest. Dark, rich pheromones fill my nostrils, salt and musk and oceanic wilderness, blasting life into my senses.

Every cell within my body buzzes with yearning and delight, his scent a feast for my olfactory system.

"Hush, little mama. I'm here."

When did I start crying? Why am I crying?

Why won't my arm lift to touch his handsome face?

The world shifts and water patters against a hard surface seconds before he sets me in his lap.

"It's okay, Duri. We're safe. Let me take care of you."

I nod, rubbing my face against his chest. My teeth ache, wanting to sink into the flesh of his pectoral, but I don't have the energy to fulfill even that wish. Gentle fingers tilt my chin and the lip of a bottle presses against my mouth. I obey his silent command and sip the liquid, surprised to find it slightly sweet and yet bitter.

His purr turns me into a puddle of goo. I have no defenses against him, nor do I wish to build any.

We need him, both myself and my babe. She jerks and thumps my internal organs, almost as though she leaps in joy at his mere presence.

When my stomach tightens and warns of nausea, I turn my face back into his chest. He slips two fingers into the space and presses a morsel of food against my lips. I take it, saliva instantly flooding my mouth at the intense flavor of jerky, and I chew the bite with more relish than I intend.

Cahress groans and drops his chin to my head for half a second before encompassing me in his strong arms.

"You're killing me with that dainty purr of yours. I want to knot you, right here, right now."

Gods, I want that too. Slick pools in my pants, evidence of my need, but reminding me of how filthy I am.

I tilt my head and meet bright white-blue eyes. "Please?"

Callused digits lift the hem of my shirt and pull it over my head, ignoring the buttons completely. He snaps the front fastener on my bra open and carefully slides the material off my arms.

"Soon, little mama."

Lust shines from his eyes, but his pupils don't dilate. Memory serves me the vision of him naked and feral, his irises swallowed up by his pupils.

When I open my mouth to respond, he pops another bite of food into it and weaves his digits into my hair. Cradling my scalp like I'm the most precious thing in the universe, his other hand caresses my shoulder and slides down my arm, bypassing my throbbing breasts and joining my hand as it rests against my lower abdomen.

The moment his palm settles on my burgeoning womb, the life within bops tiny limbs against it.

Every ounce of peace and joy I sent him rises into the invisible cocoon of intimacy surrounding us. Awe and delight morphs his otherworldly features, his ears perking and whiskers lifting as a smile reveals straight, white, sharp teeth. My focus catches on the strip of fabric under his nose, but he speaks before I can ask him what it is.

"She's so tiny."

I blink up at him in surprise.

"I... I haven't told anyone the gender. How do you know?"

He tilts his head.

"Hmm. Instincts, maybe?"

"You've already bonded with her, haven't you?"

"Yes. She's mine, just as you are."

My heart melts along with my bones.

He shoves another strip of jerky into my mouth and unbuckles my pants. An odd sound shoots from my chest when he sets me on my feet. I almost choke on the food in my mouth as my furious growl pierces my ears.

He smirks, a grin tugging at his lips as he slides my trousers off. Without preamble, he peels the failed feminine pad from my womanhood, shucks his own shorts off, and picks me up again as though I weigh nothing. Before I finish chewing the jerky, he steps into the shower and closes the stall door.

Warm water cascades over both of us, invigorating my frigid flesh.

With little room to move, Cahress wedges his shoulders into the corner and lowers himself onto his butt, resting his tail along the wall and propping me sideways over his crossed legs. His turgid length presses against my bottom and the back of my thigh, tempting me to reach down and inspect the knobs protruding from his shaft.

He gathers my wrists in one of his hands and holds them over my head.

"No, Duri. I'll lose control if you touch me."

His rough digits trace and tease my front, flicking my nipples and hefting my heavy breasts in his palm before sinking lower and exploring the stretched flesh of my stomach. When he continues lower, heat throbs in my core and slick seeps from my folds.

Agitation grows behind my sternum as the soap cycle begins, masking his delicious pheromones.

His purr strengthens, whisking away all hints of frustration.

Lust coils deep in my abdomen when he parts my knees and glides his massive palm up my inner thigh. Need shakes my legs and turns my breathing ragged.

He teases the crease where my thighs meet my torso, avoiding my needy womanhood, but so tantalizingly close I feel myself swell and ripen.

"Take out the plug, Duri. If I touch you there, I won't stop."

A new voice of evil cackles in my mind, my omega self enjoying her power over him, but embarrassment heats my cheeks.

"Close your eyes?"

He nods his understanding, going a step further. Both of his hands cradle my head and he leans over, tucking his face in my wet locks. Although the position is weird, I reach down and extract the cotton from my channel, my breaths ragged as my insides flutter at the stimulation.

"Where do I...?"

"Corner. I'll put it in the trash receptacle later."

I nod and toss it into the far corner.

"Done?"

I nod again, mostly mortified despite my body begging for our joining.

He straightens his spine and resumes teasing me under the guise of washing me. When he doesn't restrain my hands, I lay a tentative palm on his chest.

The shower moves to the rinse cycle. Heat swirls both within the enclosed space and within my veins, one soothing while the other consumes.

When the water turns off, my alpha rises to his feet with me in his arms, aweing me with his strength. The dry cycle blasts hot air over our flesh, but I shiver in need.

So caught up in the view of his thick beard and strong neck I don't realize he crossed the room, I blink in confusion when he sits me on the bed.

"Make a nest, Duri."

Faint hints of other alphas waft up from the bare mattress, tainted by my dirty clothes, the pheromones accosting my sensitive senses. I study Cahress' pale blue eyes and facial hair, angry to have so much distance between us.

"What is that?" I point to the fabric clinging to his whiskers.

"It blocks pheromones."

"Take it off. Please?"

His brows scrunch and he steps closer, trailing a thumb over my bruised cheek.

"Still such a polite little omega. I'll take it off after you make us a proper nest."

My core throbs a complaint.

"I want you more than I want a nest. I need you, Cahress."

He sucks in air through his nose, filling his lungs so full his chest expands.

"The things I want to do to you... make a nest, so we can properly enjoy one another."

My lips part to ask him to knot me *right now*, but he reaches behind me and drapes a soft, fluffy blanket over my shoulders.

A need so profound my bones ache sweeps through me. He reaches behind me again and pulls another blanket into my lap.

"Nest. Now."

My fingers knead the silky fabric for a moment, logical thought fighting for control before basal needs take over. I crawl onto the bed and sink my hands into the neatly folded stack of materials, creating havoc where order once stood. I rub each blanket against my cheek, checking the scent and rating the softness.

I create three mounds of fabric, sorting them according to their ranking, and pull the pillows against my chest one at a time. Each one gets a solid hug, infusing my pheromones into the material and testing the fullness of the stuffing.

My spine aches from the extra weight of my midsection as I crawl around on the bed, but the intermittent thumping of knees and elbows against my ribs makes it worth it, and when the pillows create a ring of comfort around where I intend to fully accept my mate, I sit back on my heels and rest my stomach on my thighs for a moment.

Unable to leave my nest incomplete, I set to work, creating a jumble of pillows and blankets higher on one side than the other and spreading the softest quilt overtop it. Plopping my rear in the center, I pull the thinnest sheet over my head and settle back into the mound of blankets, wiggling and shifting the materials underneath me until it fits the shape of my body.

Cocooned in cloth and propped up so my weight remains on my tailbone instead of my spine, I sigh in pleasure and tuck the left side of the sheet under the outside of the nest before peeling open the right side.

Pushing up into a sitting position, I wrap my hand around the thickest forearm I've ever seen, enjoying the softness of his fur as I pull him over me. Mirth and lust play over his expression as I position him where I want him and pull the sheet over us. It catches on his tail, but I feed the edge over him until it reaches the edge of the nest. Our bodies brush against each other as I finish closing our cocoon, twisting as best as my swollen abdomen will allow and tucking the ends of the fabric under the outside of my perch, each teasing glide of flesh and fur fueling the fire in my veins.

My legs wrap around the outside of his thighs as I fill my hands with the soft pelt over his shoulders. Between the lust thumping through me and the embarrassment at my bold actions, my cheeks flame hotter than ever before.

"Fucking hell, you're perfection."

Woven within his resonant purr, I almost miss the reverent words as he lowers his head. Before his lips touch mine, I reach for the white fabric under his nose.

He grabs my wrist and presses it into the nest beside my head.

"Not yet, little mama. Your first kiss should be sweet and sensual."

And with that, he closes the distance between our mouths, brushing his surprisingly soft lips along mine and tickling my face with his whiskers and beard, before stealing my breath with the slow sweep of his tongue. My teeth part on a gasp, giving him access to my depths, and he explores with such gentle demand I offer him more and more until I want nothing else but to kiss him forever.

He tilts his hips, nestling the underside of his shaft within my slick drenched labia. With a gentle thrust, he weaves a cocoon of lust around my entire body, the intimate dance of our tongues emphasizing the glide of his cock along my folds.

The smooth flesh of his cockhead slips over my stiff clit, the sensation breathtaking. He takes advantage, nipping my bottom lip and diving deeper into my mouth.

His nodes scrape through my entire slit, teasing my entrance and pushing me perilously close to orgasm. My legs jerk and back arches as I gasp in response to the zing of pleasure racing up my spine.

He ends his thrust centimeters before his first nodule mashes the bundle of nerves at the top of my sex. A whine leaks from my throat. He swallows it with a heady hum, drowning me in his deep vibration as his shaft runs the opposite direction through my folds.

He sweeps his tongue along mine and drives his hips forward. Streaks of beautiful agony shoot into my abdomen as his cock's protrusions grind over my clit, infecting every nerve ending I possess and catapulting me into a soul shattering orgasm. Before I recover, he fits the tip of his cock to my opening, his purr dropping an octave as my slick gushes out from between us and coats his cock.

The stretch as he pushes his tip into me hurts so good, I sob into his mouth, losing my senses as another orgasm steals through me.

He continues his slow, sensual assault until my lungs ache and my head spins from lack of air. I strain to accept each nodule, the matching top and bottom pairs grinding against erogenous zones I never imagined existed.

By the time he fully seats himself, nothing remains outside of this moment. Nothing matters more than being joined with him in all ways possible.

When he lifts his head and nips my bottom lip again, I rip the strip of fabric off his whiskers and sink my teeth into his neck, stretching and biting closer to his chin than his shoulder. My taste buds explode with his metallic, wild flavor and my muscles convulse through another release, causing slick to burst from between our joined body. With lewd sounds echoing in my ears, I suffer a splendid rending of my heart, half of the theoretical organ leaving my chest to settle within his. Our bond widens, growing in both strength and light.

For a moment, time stands still.

Thick fingers weave into my hair and yank my face away from his throat while his massive cock pistons in and out of my body. Amidst squeals and squelching, his growl arrows through my senses and his teeth pierce my shoulder, completing the excruciating bliss as our hearts fully merge.

His knot expands, reorganizing my insides, torturing my G-spot with intense pressure. I shatter yet again, clamping down on his intrusion as his shaft jerks and fulfills my womb's hunger, our bodies locked together, preventing his seed from escaping.

Utterly worn out and completely content, I float in the waves of Cahress' peaceful ocean, lending my own pleased purring into the song of our joining.

Hidden in my nest and safe with my alpha, I slip into slumber with a smile on my face and a hand on my belly.

Chapter Twenty

Cahress

Extracting my teeth from her shoulder, I lick up the mess and trace my finger around the wound. I should have been gentler, taken greater care with her, but her responsiveness stripped away any semblance of control from me. She turned me into an animalistic beast ruled by need and instinct.

I can't find it in me to regret how we came together, though. Every moment, every sound she made, every touch was perfect. She's mine.

My arms shake from holding myself up and my jaw aches from gritting my teeth in rapture. She shifts in her sleep, coaxing another wave of euphoria from my tip as her insides squeeze my knot.

I nuzzle the top of her head, intrigued by our size difference despite the discomfort in my spine from bending to reach her. After filling my lungs with her sweet perfume, I strengthen my purr and slide my arm under her shoulders, praying I don't disturb her sleep. The exhaustion emanating from her won't go away so easily.

I look forward to pampering her and ushering her to full health. I want to show her how much I love and cherish her.

She sighs when I straighten her left leg, moving it so I don't crush it when I roll. The top sheet of our nest causes tiny zaps of static electricity as my fur rubs against it, but I don't feel it through my dense undercoat. Holding her close, I settle onto my side and gather the bottom layers of nest against my lifemate's back, propping her on her side with the mound of fabric. She sighs again and snuggles closer, her left forearm wedging between her breasts, making them pillow against my ribs in the most enticing way. Her rounded belly presses against my stomach, occasionally jerking as the life within tumbles about.

Even those tiny movements vibrate through my squished shaft, pulling another release from my balls.

I trace the muscles of her arm and the ridges of her spine, unable to keep my hands off her. For hours, I lay in mesmerized awe, wondering how in the hell I got so lucky. Wanting to remember every second of our first joining as marked lifemates, I fight my exhaustion until my body's needs win. My eyelids become too heavy to keep raised, so I give in, letting them close and drifting into a sleep deeper than any I've had in years.

"Cahress?"

Duri's throaty yet hesitant inquiry jerks me awake. I check her expression, noting her still-blown pupils, and run my hands over every reachable inch of her, needing to confirm she's alright. My knot surges back to full engorgement, the slow deflation ending as the movements highlight the tight, hot grip her body has on mine.

Finished with my inspection, I drop my head back to the pillow and hum an ascending note in response to her question.

"It hurts."

Her words pop the bubble of my satiated stupor.

"What hurts?"

"I... I need to..." her face turns so deep a red the bruise on her cheek almost disappears in the blush. What could she possibly be embarrassed about when I'm seated so firmly inside her?

Oh.

"You need the relief port?"

She nods and tucks her face against my chest.

"It's okay, Duri. There's nothing to be embarrassed about. I'll take care of you."

Her balled fists and tight muscles relay how much she's straining to accept my offering.

Gritting my teeth and forcing a soothing purr from my chest, I reach down between us and pinch the flesh connecting my balls to my groin. A barrage of white-hot streaks of agony shoot into my torso and down my legs, but I squeeze harder, until my knot softens in response.

I mask my pain by offering her comfort. She aims wide eyes at me, confusion and shock alternating through her expression.

Just before my knot slips free, I push her onto her back. With an almost audible pop, it deflates. I yank my shaft free and swoop down her body.

Led by a need too fierce to deny, I press her legs down on either side of her belly and lap at her gushing pussy, curling my tongue and growling in delight. My right hand leaves her knee and cups the excess in my palm and ferries it to her lips.

Wide eyes meet mine, nothing but black pupils showing as she swallows our mixed essences. As the flow ebbs to a trickle, I tell myself to stop licking her, but she tastes so sweet my tongue refuses to stop.

Feminine fingers grab fistfuls of my hair and tug. I growl and consume the resulting slick.

Her whine only increases my enthusiasm. She tenses and wraps her unattended leg over my shoulder. I snarl in victory as she pulses in release, her squirming giving way to a full body convulsion.

Still panting and flushed, she grabs my shoulders, pushing me away but holding my fur in her fists.

Panic fills her features, so I scoop her up and rise, ruining our nest. Two seconds later, I set her in front of the relief port, ensuring she has her balance before I release her.

"Be quick. I don't have the patience to keep my hands off you for very long."

She nods and gets to business, glancing over her shoulder at me as she lifts the port from its holster. Understanding her blush, I turn and busy myself with gathering food and water, placing it within easy reach beside the bed. When the port snaps back into place, I wrap my arms around her from behind and span my hands over the bottom of her belly.

"Better?"

She nods but doesn't speak. I turn her around by her shoulders and lose the ability to speak.

Too gorgeous for words, her tussled hair and pink skin calls for me to gather her close, but her pale blue eyes steal my breath.

Our joining caused many changes. My heart lives to worship hers, our souls forever merged. I'll never be the same.

And neither will she. Her irises shine with the same luminescence as mine, displaying just how concrete and profound our lifemating bond runs.

Capturing her lips in a heated kiss, I tilt her head and pour my joy into the joining of our mouths. When I lift my head, her pupils threaten to swallow the sparkling blue of her irises.

"Gods, you are perfection."

Her brows crease despite the lifting of her lips. I sidestep, pulling her with me, and rotate her toward the mirror. Her gasp of surprise fills me with the need to comfort her, so my hands roam over her naked flesh.

"How?"

"You've never seen a lifemated pair?"

"I... I suppose not. Is this normal?"

The desire to cremate every individual who ever denied her access to knowledge, anyone who ever stopped her from living her life to the fullest, and all idiots in her society who thought suppressing her natural omega tendencies would be beneficial—in my mind, I decimate every male figure she knew before me.

Every little nuance of the censorship her society forced on her flits through my memory— the way she was treated during her first and only heat, her embarrassment over anything remotely sexual, her sadness for her best friends' plight—it all surges through me and fills me with hatred.

Her pupils shrink and face goes pale.

"I-I'm sorry. I didn't mean to make you mad."

If I could cut out my own larynx to punish myself for scaring her, I would, but I'd ruin any chance of a happy future with her.

I soften my growl and rest my chin on the top of her head, rubbing the goosebumps from her arms.

"I'm not mad at you, little mama. I'm sorry I got carried away."

After a moment of searching my reflection, she nods and rests her hand over mine.

"Okay, but why are you mad?"

"Because you deserve so much better than what life has thrown at you. From now on, I plan to be by your side, giving you everything an omega could ever dream of having."

Her lips lift in an off-centered smile, tears gleaming in her beautiful blue eyes.

"You already have, Cahress."

I pick her up and cradle her to my chest before stalking back to the bed.

"Not yet. There's still so much I want to do to you."

Her scent thickens, her lust skyrocketing the temperature within the tent until I envision steam wafting from her tempting flesh.

"Fix our nest, so I can ravage you the way you deserve."

A single tear slips down her face. I wipe it away with my thumb.

"I love you, Cahress."

I bend down and press my forehead to hers, opening the bond between us and offering her all the honesty I possess.

"And I love you, Duri. Forever."

Our lips join, soft and sweet at first, but I deepen the kiss as her luscious scent overrides my senses. I pour my love into her mouth, relaying the depths of my devotion.

I force myself to back away. A whine leaks from her throat before she clamps a hand over her mouth, her eyes blinking at me in mortification. Wrapping my digits around her dainty wrist, I pull her hand away.

"Don't hide from me. I love how you respond."

She searches my expression and thinks for a moment before surprising me with an almost sly smile.

"I know. It's just hard to not be surprised by my own responses. I always dreamed there was more to life than marrying for status, but I never imagined it would be this..."

After struggling a few seconds, she shakes her head and reaches up to hook a hand behind my neck.

"I never actually believed I could have a happily ever after, but I think I've found it. With you."

She initiates a kiss for the first time, bringing me to my literal knees with the utter raw, sweet sensuality only she possesses. When she pulls away, I let her, only so I don't drag her to the floor and rut her with the raging greed of an alpha beast.

"Fix the nest before I knot you on the floor."

Her breathing quickens, the beautiful pink of her nipples darkening as the peaks harden.

"You can do that?"

I chuckle.

"Little mama, I could rut you anywhere. In fact, I plan to, when you're back at top health. Right now, though, you need the comfort of your nest."

She dips her chin, trying to hide the smile playing on her lips, turning her attention to fixing the nest. As she works, I pop a bite of food into her mouth, risking the fury of interrupting a pregnant omega as she builds her sacred refuge, needing to ensure she's well cared for.

By the time she finishes primping, kneading, and fluffing, she's eaten half a meal but no water. When she pulls me into her nest and pushes me onto my back, I wait until she settles against me, enjoying her sigh of satisfaction, before reaching out and dragging the water sack closer. She accepts the hose and sips with lackluster interest until I take it away.

"Cahress?"

Yet again, she flays me with her tentative innocence.

"Yes, Duri?"

"How can I feel so content and scared at the same time?"

She's right. Fear wafts from her, an almost abstract cloud of worry emanating from deep within her soul.

"Why are you scared?"

"What if we never find Seung?"

Self-loathing tightens my guts.

"Shit, I didn't realize you thought… Duri, he was in the group of alphas who fought free with me."

Her entire body stiffens.

Chapter Twenty-One

Duri

Wait, what? Seung was within sight, and I didn't even notice?

Heat creeps up my neck as I remember the reason why: Cahress in all his naked glory, hard and gleaming in the sunlight, his muscles pumped from fighting his way free.

"I... didn't see him."

"And I didn't even think to bring it up. I'm sorry. I could have stopped you from worrying."

"It's my fault. I should have seen him."

A warm thumb tilts my chin up to meet his gaze.

"I only had eyes for you, as well. There's no shame in what's between us. You couldn't help focusing on me any more than I could on you. We're lifemates. He'll understand."

How does he know exactly what to say to ease my worry? How does he know that despite me preparing to separate from my lifelong best friend for years, I'm still not ready for it? That the worst thing I could ever suffer would be Seung's anger or disappointment?

He moves his hand to my hair, pushing it from my face and running his fingers along my scalp over and over until all traces of stress seep away.

"Duri, I *see* you. I feel you. You're a part of me. You'll never be alone again. Never have to suffer on your own. Never need to worry about the future. You and yours are mine now."

His hand drifts down my neck, sending shivers down my spine as he ghosts the rough pad of his finger over the mark his teeth left in my shoulder, and continues downward to caress my round belly.

"I'll love her as though I sired her. I already do. I can't wait to pamper her through her early years. To watch her grow. To protect her. To cherish her as I do her mother."

The mattress shakes as silent tears trail across my face, wetting my temple and his bicep tucked under my head.

"I can't wait to introduce her to our family."

My hiccup almost ruins my attempt to respond.

"Family?"

"Yes. My mother and sisters, Seung, my teammates, and the rest of the fleet. She'll be a treasured addition."

I lose it. Sobs wrench my chest as my entire body shakes, overwhelming joy snatching my control from me. His words break me to pieces, destroying every ounce of doubt I cultivated throughout my life, and rebuild me into someone I never dreamed I could be.

"It's okay, little mama. I've got you. I'll always have you."

When I finally calm down, my head pounds and fatigue weighs down my limbs, but I meet pale blue eyes and smile my gratitude. He returns the sentiment, purring and wiping my face. After sweeping his lips over my hairline, he sticks the water straw between my teeth and pulls me closer to him.

"Sleep for a while, so I can fulfill my promise."

"Which promise?"

"The one where I teach you all about the joys of mating."

With a smile on my face and a peace more profound than the vastness of space, I slip into sleep, knowing without a doubt that when I wake, he'll be by my side, ready to sate my every need.

***

I pull the bottom hem of my shirt down and wish I could somehow get closer to Cahress, even though he hugs me to his side. After several days of hiding in our den, I no longer feel on the verge of collapse, but my emotions swing from one extreme to the other so quickly my head spins.

Foreign pheromones assault my nostrils as Cahress leads me into the larger tent on the other side of the hill. A vague sense of deja'vu plagues me, but no concrete memories rise until we step into a large, white room containing rows of hospital gurneys.

The last time I was here, I was so hyper fixated on sending support through our incomplete lifemating bond I couldn't focus on my surroundings.

Three alphas stand against the far wall. My feet refuse to move another step forward despite the long distance between us. For a few seconds, all I can do is stand frozen in place before recognition sets in.

Seung, Commander Ru'en, and Jokur wait for us near the tent's other exit. Both of my alpha's teammates wear the same black suits they wore last time I saw them, sans their masks. I fight against nausea as their scent reaches my nose.

Even Seung's pheromones sit heavy in my nostrils, not quite unpleasant, but also wrong enough to make me want to curl my nose. I refrain, meeting my best friend's light brown eyes as I wrap my arms around Cahress' midsection.

A surge of emotion moves my feet forward. Cahress holds me back, keeping me plastered to his side. He doesn't budge, and I don't fight, my arms remaining around his middle.

Talk about mixed signals.

"Are you okay?"

Seung's smooth voice fills my eyes with tears.

"Oh, yes. I'm more than okay, except I feel horrible for not seeing you sooner."

The lines around his eyes disappear and his shoulders, which once seemed so impressive but now look too slim compared to Cahress', relax.

"I think you had better things to think about. Stop worrying about me, sprite."

"I can't help it. After everything you've been through—"

"No. After everything *we've* been through. Don't discount yourself, Duri. You always have, I was just too selfish to see it. I'm happy to see you so happy."

"I... but what about you?"

The barest hint of a smile curves his mouth.

"You did what you set out to do forever ago, even if you didn't do it how you meant to."

"What do you mean?"

"I'm off that wretched planet. I'm in a much better place, somewhere I can find acceptance. So, thank you, sprite."

Cahress' arm tightens around me, a warning creeping into his quiet purr. His possessiveness heats my veins, the incessant throbbing of my clit intensifying despite how sore I am from his vigorous claiming.

Seung's smile widens.

"Where's the other two?"

I glance up at the tense set of my lifemate's shoulders and squeeze, needing to comfort him.

"They led another team back to the facility you broke out of but haven't come back. As soon as we're done here, we're heading out with Warrior Elite Team 6 and whoever else is qualified to volunteer for a search and rescue."

"Then go. Choku and Thret would have reported back if they were able."

"We're not done yet."

Agitation tightens my alpha's frame so much I worry he'll snap. Instinctual knowledge makes me press harder against him, rubbing my belly into his side, knowing the reminder of our babe will help soothe him.

"Oh? What's left to be said?"

"It wasn't an accident."

The world stands still as we try to process the information. What wasn't an accident?

"The ship didn't randomly crash on Mai'CuS. Intelligence found highly coded correspondence between two ISC branches. They coordinated the crash."

Ice congeals my blood, memories of fire and smoke, death and fear, and alphas in white hazmat suits flash through my mind's eye. The floor disappears out from under me. I brace myself, expecting to fall like always, my clumsiness a burden I unconsciously accept, but find myself tucked against a massive chest instead. His deep rumble pulls me from my misery and allows me to focus on the present.

"It isn't safe for you on Mai'CuS, so the Fleet Commander wants you to join your mother's ship in orbit. All three of you."

I don't know how to respond to his news. Hot and cold, terrified and excited, sad and happy, I burrow deeper into my lifemate's thick pelt, too busy flipping through chaos of memories to handle reality.

Instead, I focus on the secondary heartbeat within my body, reassuring myself through the precious new life I carry within my womb.

"When?"

"As soon as Duri's fit for travel."

"She needs another day or two, then."

"What about you two? Shouldn't all Warrior Elites return to base until we get better intel?"

"Everyone has, except for the party including Thret and Choku. We can't leave them out there, dead or alive."

"Those fuckers, making us all worry over them. We'll be back with them in no time," Jokur says, his voice unexpectedly lighthearted.

The shock of such gaiety lifts my face from my alpha's fur.

With one last look over his shoulder, the spotted alpha meets my lifemate's gaze. My heart skips a beat, the single glance holding enough emotions to charge the space between them.

Hidden beneath his flippant exterior lies the deep-rooted belief of finality. He doesn't expect to return.

I twist and jerk, intuition demanding I reach out to Jokur and stop him from leaving, but Cahress spins on his heel and stomps toward the exit.

"Bring them back in one piece, Commander Ru'en."

His uneven snarl arrows through my heart. He understands Jokur's hidden message.

His teammate knowingly walks to his doom.

Next in series: Freed and Filled (Warrior Elite Series Book 7)

***

Need more Duri and Cahress? Join my newsletter and enjoy a **free and filthy** _Newsletter Exclusive Bonus Scene_! You'll also get _knotty artwork, free coloring pages,_ and _much more!_

Join my Newsletter by scanning the QR code below or visit:
https://vtbonds.com/newslettersubscriber/

***

What's the best way to let me know what you think? Leave me a review! Reviews are like gold—highly sought after, useful, and extremely beautiful. Even a simple, 'I liked it,' enriches a book tenfold. I'd be forever grateful!

Keep up with V.T. Bonds

My Newsletter:
https://vtbonds.com/newslettersubscriber/

My website:
https://vtbonds.com/

Find me on:
Bookbub
Goodreads
Facebook